BAD VOODOO

TIMOTHY GRAY

iUniverse, Inc.
Bloomington

Bad Voodoo

iUniverse books may be ordered through booksellers or by contacting:

iUniverse
1663 Liberty Drive
Bloomington, IN 47403
www.iuniverse.com
1-800-Authors (1-800-288-4677)

ISBN: 978-1-4620-5497-8 (sc)
ISBN: 978-1-4620-5498-5 (e)

Printed in the United States of America

iUniverse rev. date: 1/14/2013

Prologue

"Go, boy! You ain't no help to me no more!"

Papa G didn't wait for his American friend to respond. He simply reached with his long arm across the breadth of the rusted-out Buick and gave Lenny an unceremonious shove. Lenny was hardly out the passenger's side door before Papa G had the gas pedal all the way to the floor. He took one last look through his rearview mirror at his feckless pal, still stumbling in the alley in the rooster tail of dust and gravel kicked up by the Buick, and then pressed on, eyes straight ahead.

The best he could do at this point was play cat and mouse for a few minutes with Ricardo Tandino's thugs. But he knew this deserted stretch along the city's Industrial Canal well enough to know there was no way out. He was hemmed in between water and concrete, between a channel he couldn't swim and a veritable hedgerow of warehouses and factories, most of them boarded up and long since abandoned.

If there was a plus side to this debacle, it was that his pursuers would blast right by Lenny, who meant nothing to them—or anyone, for that matter. The squirrelly little American would live to lie and cheat another day. Not so, Papa G. His luck had finally run out. Or had it? He knew he should be feeling a bigger pit in his stomach than he did. He was outnumbered. Trapped. Even if he *could* swim, the idea of retreating, of giving in to the Tandinos, was intolerable. He would rather die fighting. And something told him even death wouldn't be the end of him. Maybe that was the crank talking. Or maybe it was something else.

Up ahead, the alley split into a narrow Y, and he veered right, taking the waterside route without hesitation. He had knowingly chosen a dead end. It was time.

He skidded to a stop outside the old foundry, shuttered since the seventies, and stepped out onto the simmering blacktop. He wouldn't hide. Wouldn't take evasive action. He would face the wolves like a fellow wolf. He licked his lips, waiting.

Within seconds, a car full of Tandino's goons came hurtling down the dead-end street toward him. They were just like him, young and jacked up on God-knows-what, but he knew he was better than they were, that he owned a fate bigger than anything they could imagine. They were just worker bees, drones, middlemen at best. They followed an old man's commands—couldn't even fart without Ricardo Tandino's permission. He took orders from no one.

Papa G did a quick head count: four, including the driver. *No fair for them*, he thought and tossed his gun aside as the hard-topped Monte Carlo slid to a sideways stop in front of him with barely ten feet to spare.

Louie Tandino, Ricardo's youngest son and the golden screw-up of the most powerful crime family in New Orleans, sprang from the front seat of the passenger's side of the car.

"You're one stupid son of a bitch, you know that? Did you think we were gonna slow down for that weasel back there?"

So...the father sent his spoiled brat for me. Is that all he thinks of me?

Papa G circled round Tandino, sizing him up, as the others closed in. "You will always be a witless underachiever," he said, eyeing the twenty-something Louie.

"What?" The Tandino boy gestured wildly to the others with his dark brown eyes. "Does anybody understand this Haitian fuck?"

Jeff Sloan, Louie's inseparable friend, brandished a baseball bat in his right hand. "Not me. Dude's speaking gibberish."

"Shit, man," Louie said. "He's blacker than you, Sloan."

"And you two are vanilla wafers," Papa G shot back, not bothering to soften his accent.

In fact, Louie and Sloan each had more than a hint of color. Louie, thanks to his Italian blood, sported slicked back jet-black hair, a blue-black five o'clock shadow minutes after shaving, and a smoky olive tone.

He stood five feet eight inches—on his tiptoes. Sloan, meanwhile, topped out at closer to six feet, a couple of inches more if his woolly Afro was taken into account. Half of his lineage was African-American, the other half Irish-American, and so his skin tone split the difference, mimicking the color of hot cocoa with too much milk and not enough of the chocolate stuff.

Neither was particularly formidable. Louie had made a reputation as the Tandino with the biggest mouth—and the smallest fists. He was all bark, no bite. All talk, no action. He took care of the easy jobs, although even those he screwed up. The fact that Ricardo Tandino had sent him and his pals to make Papa G disappear spoke volumes about what the elder crime boss thought of Papa G: next to nothing. Papa G had always assumed as much. He was young and up and coming and ready to carve out his own niche in the Lower Nine, but to his enemies he was merely one of many troublesome weeds that needed to be thinned, lest he go to seed.

As for Sloan, his presence here had nothing to do with talent or muscle or even ruthlessness. He was Louie's best friend, and that was all the power he needed, apparently. The other two bruisers on either side of him, though, they would be something to contend with, especially the one with the crowbar.

"I think this freak just tried to make a joke," Louie hissed. "Sloan, you believe this guy? First he dumps his only friend in the alley. Then he gets rid of his piece, like he's gonna take us on with his bare hands. And now he's making jokes. Well, my Haitian freak, the joke's on you. The joke's on you."

Papa G opened his mouth to silence the little one, but before he could speak, he felt a crushing blow to his kidneys. He whirled around to face the crowbar-wielding attacker, a caramel-skinned Latino with lightning speed. But as soon as he did, the others were on him, raining down blows and jerking at his arms. The next thing he knew he had a man at each arm and a switchblade at his neck.

"All right, wild man," Louie spat. He was standing in front of Papa G and brandishing a silencer-loaded pistol, the barrel of which was aimed at Papa G's forehead. "We're gonna take a walk."

Papa G stood firm. None of his attackers had even an ounce of his strength, strength he'd yet to call upon. What was holding him back? Fear? Mercy? He felt strangely elated, like a dove about to take its first flight.

"Terrence," Louie said to the man with the switchblade at his neck, "make the asshole walk."

A sucker-punch to the kidneys reduced Papa G to his knees, but that didn't stop his tormentors from dragging him across the street and inside a musty stairwell. From there, they kicked and dragged him up another two flights of stairs before pausing.

"Okay, boys," Louie said. "Y'all ready to do a little urban skeet shooting? Terrence," he said, not waiting for a response, "butter him up a little more so me and Sloan don't have no troubles once we get him upstairs."

Papa G felt a searing pain in his back and then saw stars, finally succumbing to a surreal wave of disorienting darkness. When he came to, he realized they'd left the stench of urine and the dim lighting of the stairwell for a brightly lit office corridor.

"There!" said Louie, who was gripping Papa G's left arm with both of his. "First window on the left, remember?"

Sloan, who had Papa G's right arm, was sweating up a storm, and it wasn't from exertion. Papa G could smell the terror on him. Was this the first time he'd been entrusted with someone's murder? Was he used to watching from the sidelines? He was like a rookie lion tamer, shaking in front of a six-foot-four, two-hundred-forty-pound mountain of a man. He had to know Papa G could crack his skull against Louie's the moment he felt the inspiration. Louie, though, knew nothing but overconfidence.

"What do they call this freak again?" Louie said as they dragged him to the closest window.

"Papa G," Sloan said nervously.

"Papa G? What the fuck is that? You thinking about opening up your own take-and-bake pizza joint?" Louie used Papa G's head to bash open the window, kicking out the rest of the glass with his thick-soled Dock Martins. "You shouldn't have tried to move into our neighborhood," Louie said, his voice growing darker. "Everybody knows we don't tolerate bottom feeders like you. You deal, you die."

"It's nothing personal," Sloan said, laughing now. "We gotta protect the family business."

"Who's *we*?" Louie grumbled. "You ain't even *in* the family."

"Whatever, man. You know what I meant."

They're really feeling it now. They can taste it.

"You ready down there, boys?" Louie hollered down to the others.

"Ready!" the others shouted through a window three stories down. "Give us a countdown."

"Will do!" Louie hollered. "All right, Sloan. On the count of three, we give him the heave-ho. But maybe give him a little more medicine before we do, just to make sure he doesn't cause us any trouble."

Another rain of blows from Sloan's baseball bat brought Papa G to his knees.

"Adios, bottom feeder," Louie said, pulling Papa G to his feet. "Here he comes, boys. One...two...three!"

There was a moment of doubt, of butterflies-in-the-stomach unease, when Papa G, too hefty for Louie and Sloan, got hung up in the window, the shards digging deep into his thigh. But time, moving like a jitterbug before, slowed until it was meaningless the second he felt himself dropping. The pain in his kidneys and in his skull, already fading, was replaced by exhilaration as he watched the fourth and then the third floor streak by. Then he saw two barrels flashing with fire from the second-story window. Before he could react, his body absorbed multiple concussions so powerful they knocked the wind out of him. He felt his neck lurch, and for the first time, he became keenly aware of the pavement rising up to meet him.

And then it was over. The withering pain. The ringing in his ears. The hideous laughter above him. Everything disappeared on impact.

There was a moment of dissolution, of stunning quiet. And then he could suddenly see with his mind's eye. He was staring down at himself, a twisted heap on the pavement.

Louie and his pals were still laughing as they emerged from the stairwell.

"Goddamn," Sloan said, "the dude looks like a possum on the side of the highway."

"Sure does," Louie said. "Alls he's missing is some tire tracks."

Papa G felt nothing as the Monte Carlo backed over him and then drove away. But he could hear Louie and Sloan laughing halfway down the block.

"See you in the next life, freak!"

He lay still, waiting, listening, aware of something pounding in the distance. Was it a trawler dredging the canal? A jackhammer somewhere nearby? No, it was something closer. Something he could feel inside of him, like a rising tremor, like his own voice calling out to him.

He jerked upright and clutched at his heart, which was still beating out a steady rhythm of eighty beats per minute.

"*Gede Nimbo*," he whispered, practically choking on the words.

He pawed gingerly at his chest and abdomen, where the bullets had pounded his flesh; at his thigh, where shards from the broken window had cut him artery-deep; and finally at his back, where surely he would find dislodged bones or a mess of pulpy flesh— tangible evidence of the car that had just run over him. He found nothing but bruises and a smattering of insignificant welts. He was battered. Still bathed in pain. But whole. And unharmed.

Papa G stood up tentatively and brushed himself off, all the while staring up at the fifth story window, incredulous. He reached inside his torn silk shirt, inside the secret pouch held snugly against his ribs, and felt for it, so familiar, worn so soft and smooth it was hard to imagine he'd ever lived without it. And as he retrieved it from the pouch and held it before his eyes, a grin spread across his face. He had taken all that Ricardo Tandino's thugs could dish out—and survived. He would need time, and more practice, for surely a war like the one he envisioned could not be hastily waged, much less won. He would need to disappear, to play along, for now, with what everyone would assume was the truth: that Papa G was dead. Finally, he would need to build a gang—no, an *army*—willing to die for him, again and again, if need be.

But he would return someday to New Orleans. And he would have his revenge.

Chapter 1

Ten years later...August 2005

Detective John O'Meara killed the engine of his prehistoric Chevy Bel Air, and the closest thing he had to a girlfriend hiccupped twice before falling silent.

"Shut up," he said, stepping from the steamy confines of American metal into the sweatbox of another sultry August morning in New Orleans.

It was hurricane season once again in the Gulf, and the detective found himself wincing from the glare coming off the potholed parking lot of the fifth district police station. Two things he didn't do well—hangovers and first-thing-in-the-morning meetings—had converged to torture him simultaneously. The hangover was his fault: he'd had one too many Blackened Voodoos last night, and no amount of kneeling before the porcelain altar was going to erase that fact. He would have to sweat off his overindulgence one cotton-mouthed hour at a time.

But the morning meeting was beyond his control. Captain James Whiting, fearless leader of the fifth district, had called an all-hands-on-deck meeting, something reserved only for serious trouble, the kind of trouble now facing O'Meara and his colleagues. One of their own had gone missing, first disappearing three days ago, and the captain, after flying by the seat of his pants for the last couple of days, had decided it was time to cobble together a comprehensive plan to find the missing officer. Captain Whiting was no doubt facing all kinds of pressure—from his superiors, from the media, from the family of the missing officer—but O'Meara knew his captain well and knew that what was getting to Whiting the most was the simple fact that one of his men was in trouble. Whiting seemed able to tolerate just about anything else.

The missing officer was one Max Schaeffer, a detective who worked alongside O'Meara and the others in narcotics. Schaeffer was relatively young and inexperienced, but he was streetwise and New-Orleans-wise. He had grown up less than thirty blocks away in the Lower Ninth Ward, another hard-luck African-American kid in a city full of them. But he had somehow managed to overcome the lousy odds of someone growing up without a father or health insurance or a refrigerator full of food. He'd been with the force three years and had been coming up on his annual review when he simply didn't show up for work one day. A panicked call from his wife that morning had yielded the news that he hadn't come home the night before.

At first, a handful in the department had suggested the usual culprits. Schaeffer had a mortgage to pay and three young children to feed. Maybe the daily grind had ground him down. Or maybe he was in the middle of an indiscretion gone horribly wrong. Maybe the pressure of being hated by half the city and distrusted by the other half had finally fractured his psyche. Had he been won over by the very drug dealers he was supposed to be putting behind bars? If so, he wouldn't be the first cop in town to try to steal a piece of the action. But such scenarios, however plausible in theory, just didn't hold up to scrutiny, especially if those doing the scrutinizing knew Schaeffer. He was young, yes. But every bit as steady as veterans with a decade of experience for every year he had.

This morning's meeting would pool the department's always stretched-thin resources, putting an organized veneer on an impossibly messy situation. For, although there was an official playbook to put into action, the officers at the fifth precinct were already doing everything possible.

O'Meara entered the briefing room and found every seat taken and many of the prime spots along the back wall already spoken for, as well. Captain Whiting was making his way toward the front of the room, where a modest oak podium stood, flanked by a dry eraser board and a blank screen. The room was stuffy, as usual, which was no surprise, considering it was crammed with dozens of officers and only boasted two overhead AC vents, limply sputtering cool air from the 1970s-era ceiling tiles. O'Meara exchanged nods with his best friend in the department, Billy Thune, who was seated near the front, and then found a place to stand against the back wall, near the exit.

"All right," Captain Whiting said from the podium in a voice that sounded like it had been run through a coffee grinder, "let's get started."

As far as O'Meara knew, the captain had never smoked a cigarette in his life. But he still found a way to sound like someone just a few Marlboros away from needing a breathing tube, tracheotomy, or some other medical intervention to keep him upright. Kindhearted and fair-minded, he sported a mostly bald head with a luminous patina—and a pair of ears worthy of a Disney character. Thanks to his perpetually gravelly voice, he didn't talk so much as he croaked. And those under him had learned to keep it zipped while he spoke, both for sympathetic and practical reasons. It was that or wait for him to explain himself all over again.

"This is what we know so far about Officer Schaeffer's disappearance," the captain said and launched into a PowerPoint presentation on the missing detective, complete with an hour-by-hour synopsis of the hours leading up to his disappearance and a citywide map, broken into color-coded grids, indicating the last few locations he'd been seen.

As O'Meara glanced around the room and studied his fellow officers, he didn't see much in the way of gritty determination or dogged optimism. Max Schaeffer had been gone three days. If he'd left any kind of a trail, it was growing colder by the minute.

This meeting, as far as O'Meara was concerned, was all for show. It was designed to make everybody involved, from Schaeffer's distraught family to the mayor himself, feel like *something* was being done. But the only thing worth doing—and the only thing O'Meara knew how to do—was to hit the pavement. Anything else, especially if it smelled like PR, was a waste of time.

As soon as he'd finished with his planned remarks, Captain Whiting began quizzing his officers, asking various detectives on various beats about the latest news. What did their sources have to say? Did they have any leads worth pursuing? How could the rest of the department assist them?

Detective O'Meara had nearly dozed off, arms folded, spine resting snugly against the back wall, when the captain called on him to speak.

"What about you, John? Anything about this case strike you as...*interesting*?"

O'Meara fought the urge to straighten himself like someone who'd just been caught napping. Instead, he casually shifted his weight from one foot to the other and then paused to mull over the question.

Interesting was a loaded word. Everybody in the department knew about O'Meara's special talent. What the captain wanted to know was if there was anything unusual about Max Schaeffer's disappearance. Had there been any furtive talk of the occult? Any oblique references to paranormal activity? If so, O'Meara would know. Because he didn't have to go looking for weird shit. In this town of aboveground crypts and belowground creeps, the underworld came to him.

And usually he got a hint of it before it arrived: a queasy feeling in his gut or a tingling sensation on his spine. He was tapped into all things uncanny. Hence his reputation for a *sick*, not a sixth, sense.

But in this case, nothing seemed out of the ordinary, aside from Schaeffer's disappearance.

"I got nothing," O'Meara finally said.

"Nothing?" Captain Whiting croaked.

O'Meara nodded thoughtfully. "Detective Schaeffer was trying to infiltrate the Tandino network, right? If I was in charge, that's the first place I'd look."

The Tandinos, led by the legendary crime boss Ricardo Tandino, were the closest thing New Orleans had to an old-school mafia family. They had their hands in everything—from real estate to riverboat casinos—and had done such a thorough job over the decades of enmeshing themselves with the city's respected politicians, judges, and businessmen and women that they were all but bulletproof. Indeed, they gave millions each year to local aid organizations, arts projects, scholarship programs, city festivals, neighborhood grants, urban beautification—the list was endless. And in return for their largesse, they earned a blind eye from law enforcement.

Everyone knew they were dirty. But no one with good taste talked about it. Even Max Schaeffer's efforts had been aimed primarily at nabbing the middlemen working for the Tandinos, not the Tandinos themselves. And he'd been forced to go about his work in a highly delicate way so as not to offend the Tandinos or their friends.

The room fell silent, and the officers that had

turned to listen to O'Meara resumed their forward gaze.

"Point noted," Captain Whiting said hoarsely. "Anybody else got any ideas?"

O'Meara stepped inside Franny's Pet Palace and frowned as the door swung closed behind him, cutting him off from the rest of a rundown commercial strip in the Ninth Ward. If the air outside reeked of diesel fumes and broiling blacktop, the air inside was nothing but organic soup, a pungent gumbo of gerbil chow, fish funk, and cat crap.

Lenny, as usual, was in the back corner of the store, where he was scrubbing the inside of an empty fish tank in the relative darkness of the fish aisle. The area was lit only by the fluorescent tube lights of the fish tanks, ostensibly to put the spotlight on the fish but more likely so that corner of the store didn't have to be kept as clean as the rest. In any case, half the tanks were empty, which meant half the lights were off.

"Lenny Pointer," O'Meara said as he stopped in front of the former convict.

Lenny looked up from his work, and his eyes, glassy a second before, started darting fearfully around the room. "Man, you on me again? Now what you want?"

O'Meara laughed once, softly and strictly with his shoulders. Lenny, whether he was having a good day or an awful one, was always alarmed at the sight of the cop responsible for busting him a decade ago. He was a teetotaler now, a former junkie and two-bit dealer turned stone cold sober. But he still had a guilty conscience, which went on display every time he jumped at the sight of O'Meara.

"Relax, Lenny. I was just in the neighborhood and thought I'd drop by."

"I was just in the neighborhood and thought I'd drop by," Lenny said, repeating the detective's words. It was a nasty habit of his: echoing everything the people around him said. "You never just drop by, man. I know you ain't here to shoot the shit. You want something. You always do."

It was true. Whenever O'Meara was digging for something, he went first to Lenny, who, since his release from prison four years ago, had become the detective's go-to rat. A native of the Lower Nine, Lenny knew everybody in the neighborhood (and half the prison population). He was a forever-flowing fount of information, even if he usually dispensed it reluctantly and in beleaguered fashion. Reluctant and beleaguered—that was Lenny. Always sporting a head-hugging shave (it was that or let the world know how far his hairline had receded already, at age twenty-nine), always staring up at his interrogators with wild, wide eyes, he had the constitution of a deer in flight. He had done his time, paid his debt to society. But he still had high blood pressure and a grab bag of nervous ticks, each the result of years of looking over his shoulder. He made amends for his past life by putting in long hours at the store, where he worked five days a week selling beta fish and other exotics to the locals. In his off hours, he could usually be found at a watering hole somewhere, sipping tea from a clear glass mug.

"You caught me," O'Meara said. "Schaeffer's still missing. I need to know the latest."

"The latest, the latest, the latest," Lenny repeated, his voice trailing off. "Listen, there ain't no latest, see? This is the second time you asked me this week, and the second time I got no answer for you." He looked nervously at his watch and then returned to scrubbing the tank, this time working with twice as much vigor. "Ain't nobody know what happened to your boy, Schaeffer. He's just gone with the wind, man."

"All right," O'Meara said. "If you see anything, talk to anybody, you know where you can reach me."

It was obvious when Lenny was pliable—and when he was too skittish to pump for information. At the moment, he seemed more anxious than normal. But that was to be expected, considering the heightened tension in the Lower Nine. People went missing all the time in New Orleans. But a cop disappearing set everyone on edge. The cops were bristly, and so were the neighbors, since jacked up cops tended to mistreat the citizenry.

"I know where I can reach you," Lenny said without lifting his head up from his work.

O'Meara nodded and left, reaching for his sunglasses as he stepped outside into the sweltering heat. His stomach felt fine. And so did his spine. But something was definitely off with the Lower Nine in general and Lenny in particular. The air was buzzing—and not in a good way.

Chapter 2

By late that afternoon, Detective O'Meara could finally feel his hangover easing its grip on him. Alcohol was still sweating from his pores, true. And his mouth felt like the Kalahari Desert. But the crushing headache was gone. As was the faint hint of nausea. The former had been replaced by a case of perma-squint, and the latter by the irresistible urge to eat something served in a greasy paper bag. All in all, he felt just shy of copasetic.

After his brief visit with Lenny, he had spent the rest of his shift canvassing the streets, staying as far away from the station as possible. It wasn't that he disliked the others back at the fifth precinct; he just couldn't stand being cooped up inside all day. His office was his reasonably spacious and slightly musty unmarked Ford sedan, not the cramped desk he'd been assigned by Captain Whiting. Instead of working the phones or answering e-mails, he made contact in the flesh, face-to-face. Of course, his method didn't always net better results. But it helped him steer clear of office politics and whatever other hazards lurked in the precinct's air-conditioned comfort.

Today's digging had produced nothing in the way of tips, honest or otherwise. But he wasn't surprised. Like Lenny, the rest of the folks in the Lower Nine claimed to know nothing of the whereabouts of Max Schaeffer. And like Lenny, they were clearly spooked. Nevertheless, the detective was determined to maintain a steady presence in the neighborhood. His was a familiar face to some of the residents, and he had just enough faith in his own charm to think he might have a shot at eventually wearing down at least one or two of them.

"Hey, sis," he said into his cell phone, not bothering to pull over. "How's life in the big city?"

A week seldom went by without a call to Payton, his kid sister, a schoolteacher who lived and taught in New York City, not far from where the two of them grew up in the Bronx. She was his only lifeline to the old neighborhood, to memories that at times felt like they belonged to someone else.

"Lousy."

It took a second for her answer to sink in. Payton was perennially, *militantly* optimistic.

"Lousy?" O'Meara asked.

"Uh-huh," his sister said, her normally sweet voice laced with melancholy.

The detective pulled over next to an old gas and sip, all boarded up, and slipped the sedan into neutral. This conversation was going to require his full attention.

"Talk to me, Payton. What's going on?"

"I don't know."

"What do you mean you don't know?"

"I mean I don't know. I don't know what's going on. Things are just...*off*."

O'Meara unscrewed the cap on a half-empty bottle of water and took a swig. "What things?" he asked, wiping his mouth dry. "Off how?"

"It's Mark."

Mark, Payton's husband of five years, was exactly the type of person O'Meara tried to avoid, whether on the job or in his personal life. A mortgage broker with a Type-A personality, Mark was always stressed out, always on the go, and always pontificating about the latest and greatest whatever. He had rubbed the detective wrong the very first time they met, which unfortunately had been at Mark and Payton's wedding—too late for O'Meara to take his sister aside and discourage her from committing the rest of her life to the guy. Was it his smug grin? Or the way his eyes were always on the move, forever searching for the next person to glad-hand, the next deal to make?

O'Meara scowled. He had never liked the man. "What's up with Mark?" he asked, trying not to sound judgmental.

"It's hard to put into words," Payton answered softly, sounding like she was on the edge of tears. "He just seems distracted. You know how busy he is. These days he's rarely home, and when he is, he seems distracted, like he's not all there."

"Are you...*connecting*?" O'Meara asked as delicately as he could before draining the last of his bottled water.

"No. And that's part of the problem. I want to have a baby."

The detective nearly choked on his water. "You... want...to have a baby?"

"Uh-huh."

He was in dangerous territory now. He would have to frame his next question carefully. "When did you two decide you wanted to become parents?"

"We didn't," Payton answered glumly. "It's all my idea. I don't know when it happened exactly, but the urge just hit, you know? I know I'm only twenty-seven, but I just feel like it's time. I'm ready."

"I'm sure you are."

"Well, ever since I started talking about it, Mark has been coming home later and later from work. Sometimes he never comes home at all. He's always flying to these conferences. Even when he's home, he's on the phone with work or staring at his laptop."

"I see." O'Meara had seen this kind of behavior before. He hoped Mark was just suffering pre-fatherhood jitters. But it was possible he was distracting himself with something other than work. "Listen, kid, Mark's probably just a little nervous. You know how guys are. Give him time to come around. Before you know it, he'll be ready to—"

The detective's radio came alive with the dispatcher's voice back at the station. All available units were being directed to a posh address in the Garden District, where Billy Thune and another officer were already on the scene.

"I have to go, Payton. Hang in there, okay?"

"Okay," his kid sister said in an uncharacteristically diminutive voice.

O'Meara clicked off his cell phone and jammed the sedan into drive.

He then dialed Billy. "What am I walking into?"

"Still assessing the situation," Billy answered breathlessly. "Got a wounded shooter holed up inside. Sounds like Tony Tandino's been hit, along with a couple of his goons. It's looking like a bloodbath. Gotta run."

A bloodbath? Anthony Tandino was Ricardo's prized nephew and, though only in his late twenties, one of the most respected—and powerful—members of the family. If he was hurt, or worse, there would be hell to pay.

By the time O'Meara arrived at the Greek-columned townhouse, Billy and several others had already used yellow tape to cordon off the sidewalk near the front gate. Three squad cars and one unmarked car were parked out front along the wrought-iron fence, which stood only four feet tall but was topped with ivory leaf-shaped spikes.

A young woman splattered with blood was bundled in a blanket and leaning against the side of Billy's squad car. She took a drag from a cigarette, glanced at O'Meara as he got out of his sedan, and then looked away, shivering as she exhaled.

Billy was just finishing up a call on his cell phone and met O'Meara on the other side of the street, where O'Meara had parked. The closest thing he had to a partner, Billy was everything O'Meara wasn't:

punctual, respectful toward authority, and a team player. A handsome African-American with a chiseled jaw line and an athletic build, he did everything by the book, but he thought for himself and was anything but a suck-up. Thus he had earned O'Meara's respect since joining the narcotics beat seven years earlier. If he could tolerate O'Meara's unorthodox style, O'Meara was more than happy to be paired with him on assignments, although Billy of late seemed to be spending more time back at the station or working alongside other detectives tasked with safer assignments, a development O'Meara chalked up to the little bundle of joy growing in his wife's belly. Staci was due in a couple of weeks.

"What do we got?" O'Meara asked.

Billy nodded to the young woman leaning against his squad car. "That's Mrs. Tandino. Says her husband's dead. Same with a couple of his men."

"Is she all right?" O'Meara asked.

Bleach blond and the owner of a voluptuous figure, which was apparent even beneath the blanket, Mrs. Tandino was spattered head to toe in blood.

"Just a little shaken up, that's all."

"I take it that's not her blood."

"It's her husband's—and the shooter's. From the sounds of it, she was upstairs when the shooting started. She found a shotgun, waited in the bathroom off the master bedroom until the shooter was point blank, and then emptied both barrels into his knees, which was enough to cripple him but not enough to kill him, apparently. She tried administering CPR to her husband, but he was already gone."

"What about the shooter?"

"He's still upstairs, yammering and talking nonsense. What I don't understand is that he never identified himself."

O'Meara started to nod his head and then stopped. "Wait a second," he said, slowly cocking his head to the side. "What do you mean, he never identified himself?"

"It's Schaeffer."

O'Meara felt his skin crawl. "Max Schaeffer is our shooter?"

Billy nodded solemnly.

"What the hell is he doing shooting up the Tandinos?" O'Meara waved away the question before Billy could respond. "Never mind. I'm going in."

"Hold on," Billy said, trailing him. "We've got a SWAT team less than five minutes out."

"We might not have five minutes if he's bleeding to death," O'Meara said and ducked under the tape.

Billy started after him. "Then I'm coming with you."

O'Meara stopped and raised a hand. "No. I need you here. When the SWAT team shows up, I'll be counting on you to run interference."

Billy's jaw hardened. "Fine. But watch your back. For all we know, one of Tandino's men is still breathing and hoping to get off one last shot. And who knows what kind of mental state Schaeffer's in. He's obviously no longer playing by the rules."

"I know," O'Meara said tersely and hurried through the wrought-iron gate and up the short path to the Greek Revival townhouse.

A wide set of concrete steps, short but deep, led up to the front porch, which was dwarfed by four enormous white columns out front and the overhanging balcony above. O'Meara jogged up to the huge front door, still open, and slowed to a walk, silently removing his revolver from its shoulder holster. The wooden door and its frame, like the shutters framing the windows and the wrought-iron railing on the second-floor balcony above, were glossy black, forming a stark contrast against the mansion's white-on-white paint scheme.

Inside, the marble-tiled entryway could have passed for an art gallery, its walls hung with paintings lavishly framed and individually illuminated by unobtrusive track lighting above. Two bodies, neither moving, lay crumpled within a few feet of each other at the foot of the grand stairway leading upstairs. O'Meara paused next to a murky green glass orb, which was sitting atop a stone pedestal, and as he did, he spotted a trail of blood leading upstairs. He unlatched the safety on his gun and followed it up the stairs, gingerly stopping at the top, where Tony Tandino's dead body lay in a black pool of blood.

From there, he moved slowly and carefully down a long hallway, pausing at each doorway. The first few rooms were empty, but the final doorway revealed the dimly lit master bedroom, complete with walk-in closet, vanity, and adjoining bathroom. He entered cautiously, and there, visible through the doorway of the bathroom, was Max Schaeffer, bloodied and a ghastly shade of gray but still alive. The young officer sat with his back against the cupboards beneath the double sink, rocking quietly and mumbling something to himself, his arms wrapped tightly around his chest.

"Max?"

Schaeffer, dressed in his tattered and dirty uniform, continued to stare straight ahead, still rocking, still mumbling. His legs weren't much more than pulp, and the white tiled floor was slick with his blood.

"Max Schaeffer. We gotta get you out of here."

As O'Meara stepped closer, he noticed in Max's right hand a standard-issue handgun, which, with his arms still folded, was partially tucked behind his body. With each forward rock, its barrel showed in the late afternoon sunlight pouring through the glass-block windows framing the jetted tub on the other side of the bathroom.

Max looked up from his near-catatonic state, glassy-eyed and cadaverous, and stared right through O'Meara. "Not...coming...back..." His bloodshot eyes narrowed as he struggled to find the right word. "...*Again.*"

O'Meara was just a few feet away now. If he could distract Max or get him to focus on something else, he might be able to safely dislodge the gun, still reappearing from behind Max's back every time he rocked forward.

But before O'Meara could get any closer, Max jerked the gun up and waved it carelessly at him. "Not...coming...back...again."

O'Meara froze in his tracks. "What about your wife, Max? Your kids? They're worried sick about you. We need to get you to a hospital. *Now.*"

Max closed his eyes a moment, as if searching for a long-lost memory, and then shuddered. "I'm already dead," he said and bit down on the barrel of his revolver.

"Max, no!"

The third-year officer with a head twice as cool as veterans twice his age somehow managed to unload an entire clip into his mouth before slumping over, dead.

CHAPTER 3

Detective O'Meara spied the steeple and hurriedly squeezed the Ford sedan into a parking spot across the street. His mind was still racing, still struggling to catch up, and as he skipped up the stone steps and ducked inside the church, he realized part of him was still back in his car, turning off the ignition and slinging the keys in his hand.

"Bless me, Father, for I have..."

He saw the aerosol-like spray of blood as Max pulled the trigger.

"Do you wish to share your confession, my son?" came the voice through the window in the booth.

The detective, inhaling consciously for the first time that day, was suddenly engulfed in incense-scented memories. "My mother raised us all to be Catholic," he said. "Dad didn't care so much. He just wanted us to do the right thing. Christ, I wonder what he'd think of me now."

"What is it that you do now?"

O'Meara laughed. "Father, I'll tell you this:

there's nothing I haven't seen in twelve years with the NOPD. Cannibalism. Body parts smuggling. I've handcuffed a little old lady for sugaring her husband's cornflakes with arsenic—after her husband set out a dish of antifreeze for the neighborhood tomcat. I've seen every kind of death. From disemboweling to dismemberment. In real-time or after-the-fact. I've even watched a fellow officer go down in the line of duty. But I've never seen a dead man die before."

"A dead man...*die?*"

O'Meara shook his head slowly, still trying to make sense of it all. Somehow Max Schaeffer had bit down on his gun, pulled the trigger, and...pulled it five more times. "Trust me, Father. I've seen criminals hopped up on speedballs accomplish all kinds of crazy things. But bullets fired at close range tend to have an immediate and lasting impact on even the most altered. I mean..." O'Meara bit his lower lip and looked down at his feet, but saw nothing in the darkness. "I need some advice, Father. How would you do what I do and hold it all together?"

"Well, I don't know." The priest muffled a cough with his hand. "I suppose I would try to find a way to give back to the community, to encounter it in a more gentle way."

It was a beautiful, simple answer, and it hit O'Meara with full force.

"Thanks, Father. I'll do my best."

O'Meara was out the door earlier than usual the next morning. He had a long to-do list that a restless night of sleep had done nothing to condense. And first on that list was a follow-up call to his sister, which he would make from the midnight blue Bel Air with the windows rolled down and his foot on the accelerator.

"Payton," he said as soon as he got her voice mail, "I just wanted to check in with you and make sure you're okay. Sorry for having to interrupt our conversation yesterday. Duty called. Anyway, listen, I just wanted to make sure you're okay."

In fact, he wanted to do more than that, but he wasn't sure how to tell her what he suspected—that Mark was cheating on her—without saying it outright. There had to be a way to gently alert her to the possibility.

"I've been thinking a lot about what we talked about yesterday. I'm wondering if Mark is...maybe... keeping something to himself or...you know...hiding something." O'Meara grimaced. That was putting it too bluntly. "Maybe not hiding something, exactly. But, well...just do me a favor and keep an eye out for any unusual behavior, all right?" He frowned once more. "I'll talk to you soon."

With the call to his sister out of the way—and more or less botched—O'Meara arrived at the forensics lab ready to give his full attention to yesterday's gruesome episode.

The lab, always a cool sixty-five degrees thanks to the steadily purring AC, was empty, save for Red Haugen, forensic toxicologist and quirky dispenser of random trivia and little-known facts. Red, a fifty-five-year-old African-American with light brown skin, reddish-brown hair, and a freckled face, had a razor-sharp wit and a bone-dry sense of humor. At the moment, he was stooped over what remained of Max Schaeffer's body.

O'Meara took up a position on the other side of the exam table, opposite Red, and snapped on a pair of disposable latex gloves.

Red glanced up at him, his eyebrows arching above his safety glasses. "You planning on getting dirty, Detective?"

"Only if you need me to." O'Meara studied the remnants of red mud, now a brittle coating, on Max's right hand. It looked to be the same mud that had been caked on his torn uniform. "What do you make of that?"

"Pretty typical, especially on the outskirts of New Orleans. The soil in the city has been tamped down by heavy machinery, foot traffic—all kinds of human activity. And it has been stripped of its nutrients. What that means is that it's usually clay: gray or even blue-gray. But in rural and wild areas, the soil is significantly richer and comes in several shades, including red like this. I found it everywhere on the body, by the way, including under his fingernails."

"Can you trace it to somewhere?"

Red shrugged. "I doubt it. Too common. It's most likely from a pine grove. But it could come from a number of fairly diverse ecosystems, including a cypress swamp or even just some undeveloped patch of weeds in an abandoned lot. In any case, a dirty uniform wasn't Officer Schaeffer's biggest problem."

"What was?"

"Either he was a fan of *fugu sashimi*, or someone was spiking his orange juice."

"*Fugu sashimi*?"

"Puffer fish. His blood—what's left of it, anyway—reads like a pharmacologist's field guide. I found traces of *datura stramonium*, bufotenine, and tetrodotoxin, among other things. Tetrodotoxin is a neurotoxin that causes paralysis in its victims—and almost always kills them. The easiest way to ingest it is to bite into a contaminated slice of puffer fish. It can take as little as twenty minutes for it to go to work on your system. Starts with a tingling or numbing sensation in your lips, and before you know it, the only thing still functioning correctly is your brain. Everything else in your body is paralyzed, including your heart and lungs. You eventually stop breathing, or your heart stops beating, or both. Either way, you're toast. There's no known antidote."

"But that's not what killed him, Doc. He emptied an entire clip into his mouth."

"Well, see, that's where things get interesting." Red scratched with a gloved finger at the side of his freckled face. "Tetrodotoxin, if administered in a low enough dose, could theoretically be used as an anesthetic of sorts. You could put someone into a coma with it. Theoretically."

"But he was upright and conscious."

"That would be the atropine in his system."

"Atropine?"

"It's a tropane alkaloid, an anti-cholinergic drug."

O'Meara chuckled. "Dumb it down for me, Doc."

"Well, along with being used for its hallucinogenic

properties, it could be administered to counter a low heart rate."

O'Meara's mind raced. "So first Schaeffer eats a puffer fish, and then he takes this atropine like an antidote. But you said there's no known antidote to tetrodotoxin. How would he know how to do that? And what about the other drugs you mentioned?"

Red slowly removed his gloves and tossed them into the waste bin next to the exam table. "I can't answer your first question. As for the second one, bufotenine occurs naturally. It's an alkaloid found in the skin of a certain kind of toad. But it's been used on occasion as a street drug. Some claim it's an aphrodisiac. But most people would use it like a psychedelic. It's extremely dangerous and unpredictable. It can induce a schizophrenic episode in a matter of seconds. It can also kill you."

"And *datura*...?"

The toxicologist nodded. "*Datura stramonium* is the botanical name for jimson weed. It belongs to the nightshade family. It's an herbaceous bush with a fragrant flower. All parts, including the seeds and the leaves, are poisonous. It's been used as a hallucinogen since ancient times by various indigenous people all over the world."

"Does it grow around here?"

"Like a weed. You can find it on the side of the highway or popping up out of someone's compost pile. The seeds can stay dormant for years before germinating."

"And what's it do?"

"Well, like I said, it's a hallucinogen. Anyone

taking it wouldn't be able to differentiate between fantasy and reality. When it wears off, the user has no recollection of his experiences while on the drug."

O'Meara inhaled deeply into his diaphragm and then slowly let go a long sigh. "So who gave him this cocktail?"

"That's an excellent question, Detective. And I think your underlying supposition—that someone *gave* Officer Schaeffer the drugs—is a correct one. No one would ever voluntarily take any of these drugs, much less *all* of them."

"What the hell's a puffer fish?" Captain Whiting croaked. He was reclining behind his desk, arms folded, bald head reflecting the overhead light, ears ready for takeoff.

Seated across from the captain, O'Meara had just related Red's findings. Still mulling over a response, he was grateful when Billy Thune, the only other person attending this little powwow, answered from his chair next to O'Meara.

"You know—that fish that can puff itself up and get all spiky when threatened."

"People actually eat it?"

"It's a delicacy in Japan," Billy offered. "Posh restaurants charge a fortune for it."

"But nobody eats that shit here, right?"

"Actually," O'Meara said, "I think I've read about it being popular with the well-to-do, even here in New Orleans."

"There's the whole element of danger," Billy said.

"If the chef messes up, the diner ends up in the morgue."

"Culinary roulette," O'Meara chimed in.

"All right," the captain said, holding up a hand and frowning in disgust. "I get the picture. But Max Schaeffer's not any richer than the rest of us. What the hell's he doing eating puffer fish at some fancy sushi joint?"

O'Meara shrugged his shoulders. "That's what I'm gonna find out."

The captain leveled a skeptical gaze at O'Meara. "Have I assigned you to this case?"

"Well, no," O'Meara said, shifting in his seat. "But I thought we were all—"

"Actually, Detective, I'm putting you in charge of it. This case just took a crooked left turn. If we're wandering off-road, I want you at the wheel."

CHAPTER 4

"How come you spend so much time babying those fish? You're just going to feed them to the piranha."

Papa G looked up from his top-lit goldfish tank, its lid currently propped open, and stared impatiently at Blackendy, one of a handful of bruisers he had hired to guard him and his compound in the remote, mosquito-infested sticks west of New Orleans proper. Sometimes it frightened him that he had entrusted his security to the likes of this man, a dimwitted Creole with biceps as big as most people's thighs and an IQ inversely proportioned to his brawn. At the moment, Blackendy was seated several feet away, in the adjacent dining room, and had his sandals up on Papa G's most expensive piece of furniture, a carved mahogany dining room table.

"Because," Papa G finally answered from the living room, "we are what we eat."

Blackendy brought one of his enormous paws up

to his chin and scratched it thoughtfully, brushing aside his dreadlocks as he did. "Huh?"

Papa G sighed in exasperation. "I could drive into town and buy a dozen feeder goldfish from the pet store for practically nothing, but the fish they sell are kept in cramped, dirty tanks and are poorly fed. They're malnourished. Diseased. If I feed them to Simbi, he'll become malnourished and diseased. Do you understand? It is better for me to breed my own fish—in a clean tank, with plenty of room and good food to eat. I want them to grow healthy and strong, so Simbi can grow healthy and strong."

"He's definitely strong, man. He tried to bite off my hand the other day when you had me change his water."

"That's because you are graceless and unobservant."

Blackendy frowned. "And why you always giving him spinach and shit? I thought piranhas ate meat."

"They're omnivores. In the wild, their diet is varied according to the season. Sometimes they eat mostly vegetation. Other times they scavenge for meat."

"Like when a whole school of 'em picks clean some unlucky deer or something."

"They only rarely attack with such vigor and ferocity. If they do, it is because they are starving—or because they have been provoked."

"You make 'em sound all sweet-like."

"They are misunderstood, that is all."

"Kinda like you." Blackendy smiled widely, revealing a mouthful of braces.

Papa G laughed. Maybe the burly man with

dreadlocks wasn't so stupid after all. "Yes, my sturdy friend. Kind of like me."

Guymarc entered through the screen door on the front porch and passed Papa G on his way to the dining room. He had a folded up newspaper tucked under his right arm, the off-white color of the paper contrasting sharply with his dark mocha-colored skin. Unlike Blackendy, Guymarc appeared to understand every nuance of Papa G's operation. Papa G had met him while lying low in Haiti, and the two men had explored their mutual interest in the black arts for the better part of the last ten years. But unlike Papa G's passion, Guymarc's was unfocused and undisciplined. It seemed to be enough for him merely to practice his craft. He needed no purpose, no overarching mission.

"We made the front page," he said gruffly and tossed the newspaper onto the dining room table.

Papa G closed the lid to his goldfish tank, strode to the head of the table, and peered down at the article while resting both palms on the table's smooth mahogany surface, his hands framing the newspaper. The headline said it all:

Missing officer implicated in murder-suicide at Tandino estate

Papa G looked up to see Blackendy's eyes narrowing.

"Do you think they'll come after us?" the henchman asked.

"Who?" Papa G asked.

"The cops."

Papa G turned to Guymarc, who was shaking his head contemptuously. "Guymarc, please explain it to him."

Guymarc, dressed in a black T-shirt and black slacks and showing a week's worth of unruly stubble on his pockmarked face, stabbed a finger at the newspaper. "Nobody knows nothing. How are the cops supposed to trace this back to us? You got a cop who killed some mafia thugs and then emptied his gun into his own head. How are they gonna say we did it? How are they gonna know anything? Sure, they look after their own, but this is New Orleans. The cops *are* the bad guys, half the time. They'll be scurrying like rats to make nice with the Tandinos. A cop just killed Tony Tandino. Think about it, man. We just started a war, and it don't even involve us."

Papa G offered a courteous nod to his countryman. "Guymarc is correct. I've been dead for ten years, remember? How could I possibly have anything to do with Officer Schaeffer's murder-suicide?" He straightened, towering over the other two, even the thick-necked Blackendy. "But this is a war I very much intend to join. When he is hunted down like the squealing pig that he is, Ricardo Tandino will know exactly who it is that has come to take his life away."

Only three restaurants in New Orleans were currently licensed to serve *fugu*. And of those three, only one had served it in the last week.

"I am sorry, Detective," Takahiro, the diminutive chef at Two-Koi, said in a faint Japanese accent. "I do not recognize this man."

Detective O'Meara slipped the photo of Max Schaeffer back into his hip pocket. "Could he have ordered it to go? Over the phone, maybe?"

Takahiro motioned to the starkly appointed bistro tables behind him, each one a model of Spartan simplicity. Small votive candle. Unobtrusive cloth napkins. No tablecloth. "Nobody eats *fugu* to go. It is served as part of a four-course meal."

"I imagine the price tag for that is—"

"Two hundred dollars."

O'Meara's gaze traveled from one of the sparsely decorated tables to Takahiro, who, like the restaurant that employed him, was meticulously groomed. Not a hair was out of place; even his apron looked spotless. "Is there anybody else in town besides you and the other two licensed restaurants that serves *fugu*?"

"No. Nobody else."

"Nobody does it on the sly? You know, without a license?"

"It would not be worth the risk."

O'Meara turned to leave and then thought better of it. "Takahiro, why is *fugu* dangerous to eat only *some* of the time? Is it only poisonous if it's not cooked properly?"

"Actually, cooking does not remove the neurotoxin."

"Then how do you make it safe to eat?"

The chef paused a moment before offering an explanation. "The puffer fish is not actually poisonous. The neurotoxin comes from the shellfish it eats. The puffer fish is immune, mind you, but the neurotoxin builds up in its system, in its organs, especially its liver. We are trained to remove the organs without disturbing them. We use a special knife, a *fugu hiki*, to separate the flesh from the organs, which will contaminate the fish if the proper technique is not used."

"So the fish is only poisonous if one of the organs is nicked during cleaning?"

"Yes, that is right."

"What's it taste like?"

"It is very mild." Takahiro eyed the detective playfully. "Perhaps you would like me to prepare some for you."

O'Meara laughed quietly. "No thanks. I'm a little short on time—and cash. But tell me something: why are people willing to risk their lives for a mild-tasting fish? Shouldn't there be a bigger payoff at the end of that kind of gamble?"

"I think it is for the excitement. No one has ever been poisoned here while I have been the chef. But there is always a chance it could happen, however small. In Japan, people used to order the livers, which are considered a delicacy. But they were banned after too many customers were poisoned."

"Has anyone ever survived?"

Takahiro nodded. "Anyone poisoned must be rushed to the hospital for treatment, which I believe includes the ingestion of charcoal or carbon or something like that to absorb the neurotoxin. But sometimes it is too late, and the victim is assumed dead." The chef glanced askance at the detective. "There are also stories of people waking up just before they were to be cremated."

O'Meara grimaced. "At least they were unconscious

beforehand. Otherwise, you can just imagine the kind of—"

"Actually, if this happens to you, you are frozen, not asleep. You can think and hear and even sometimes see. But you cannot move or cry out or do anything to stop it. A survivor remembers everything."

———————

After striking out at Two-Koi, O'Meara fared no better with Max Schaeffer's doctor, who, while insisting on maintaining patient-doctor confidentiality, even in the wake of Schaeffer's death, did reveal one thing: the officer had passed his last physical with flying colors. If Schaeffer had been dabbling in exotic drugs, whether paralytic or hallucinatory, he had been doing so only very recently and unbeknownst to his doctor and everyone in the department.

All of which brought O'Meara full circle to where he had been at the beginning of the day. Thanks to Red's work in the forensics lab, he knew Schaeffer's health and state of mind at the time of his death: the officer had been strung out on hallucinogens and had somehow survived ingestion of a deadly neurotoxin. But how he'd gotten that way remained a mystery.

The bell on the door jangled as O'Meara entered Fanny's Pet Palace, and the detective, after smiling politely at the young woman at the cash register, made a beeline to the fish aisle in the back. This time, Lenny Pointer spotted O'Meara before he could surprise him.

"Man, can't you see I'm trying to work here?" Lenny was pushing a broom down the dim aisle, a cool fluorescent gleam illuminating half his face.

O'Meara ignored Lenny's manufactured indignation and, skipping the usual pointless banter, proceeded straight to the question foremost on his mind. "You ever hear of tetrodotoxin?"

Years of doing the wrong thing and hanging out with the wrong people had honed Lenny's lying skills, but O'Meara thought he noticed an awkward tick in the former convict's delivery.

"Tetro-what?" Lenny straightened, bringing the broom parallel with his body and holding himself upright with the handle.

"Tetrodotoxin. It's a neurotoxin that paralyzes its victims. You can extract it from the organs of puffer fish."

"Puffer what?"

Definitely a tick. "You're trying too hard, Lenny. Everybody knows what a puffer fish is."

"You mean that fish that blows up like a big ol' spiky balloon?"

"You got it."

"Well, I ain't never heard of no one making poison from one, if that's what you're asking."

O'Meara eyed him skeptically. "What about atropine? Ever heard of that?"

Lenny shook his head no.

"Bufotenine?"

Another shake of the head.

"How 'bout *datura stramonium*? Jimson weed. Ever hear of that?"

"Ever hear of that?" Lenny repeated. "Man, why you asking me all these questions? Course I've heard of jimson weed, man. I seen it growing in my grandma's back garden. She used to give me a penny for every one I pulled. Seen it in the alleys. In parking lots. Hell, I've seen it all around."

"You know anyone who's gone tripping with it?"

Lenny's face soured. "Not personally. But I've heard about cats trying the shit. It's a wild ride is what I hear. I wouldn't mess with it. No, sir. Besides, you know I'm clean now. Why you asking me all this?"

O'Meara considered leveling with Lenny, but then thought better of it. Best to keep him off balance. He would be more helpful if he was uncomfortable. "Just curious."

"Just curious?" Lenny repeated, clearly agitated. "Just curious?"

"Uh-huh," O'Meara said and turned to leave. "I'll see you around, Lenny."

The detective took one last look back at Lenny, who was still leaning on his broom, mouth hanging open slightly, eyes dancing nervously.

CHAPTER 5

By the end of the following day, Detective O'Meara was no further with his newly appointed case. He stopped at Captain Whiting's office on his way out and found him poring over some paperwork. The man in charge of the fifth precinct kept a tidy office, which, aside from a ficus tree in the corner and a couple of framed photos of his wife and kids on his desk, was all business. The venetian blinds on the north-facing window were almost always open, although the view of the employee parking lot wasn't exactly inspiring. The vaguely beige walls, meanwhile, were decorated only with a handful of awards.

Whiting looked up from his work. "What do you got?"

"Nothing."

The captain sighed heavily and then removed his reading glasses, setting them carefully on his desk.

"All right," he said hoarsely. "Let's review what we know so far. We know Max was trying to infiltrate the Tandino family, a job everyone else in this department was glad to see someone else doing. We know his case file was pretty much empty. The guy took horrible notes. We know he was high as a kite when he shot up Tony Tandino and his bodyguards."

"We also know somebody poisoned him with a neurotoxin," O'Meara interjected.

"Right. So we've got a drugged cop taking the law into his own hands and then for whatever reason ending his own life. The question is this: who gave him the drugs?"

O'Meara mulled over the possibilities. "It must have been someone with the Tandinos. They must have known Max was looking for a way in. Maybe Tony tried to kill him with some bad puffer fish or whatever, and maybe Max, half out of his gourd, tried to return the favor."

Captain Whiting reclined in his chair. "That still doesn't explain why Max would take his own life. He had a wife and kids waiting for him at home. He had something to live for."

"I know," O'Meara said numbly. He was still trying to erase the memory of Schaeffer's bloody suicide. "Something doesn't add up."

Neither spoke for a moment.

Finally, Whiting broke the silence. "You calling it a day?"

"Almost," O'Meara said and stood up. "But first I think I'll pay Ricardo Tandino a visit."

"Hold on," Whiting croaked, nearly jumping to his feet. "Mr. Tandino is probably still red hot over his nephew's death. The last person he wants to entertain at his home is a detective from the same precinct where Max Schaeffer worked."

"I'm sure you're right," O'Meara said, pausing in the doorway. "But sometimes people say stupid things when they're angry. Maybe Ricardo Tandino will let something slip while he's kicking me off his property."

"You're going with a backup."

"Nope. This is a social call. He won't feel threatened enough to do anything he regrets."

Captain Whiting's lips tightened around a worried frown. "You better hope so."

~~~

The Tandino family had called New Orleans home for three generations, and during that time, O'Meara figured, Ricardo Tandino and his blood relations had gotten away with murder enough times to think they were untouchable. Which they were, to a degree. How many politicians, judges, and law enforcement agents had they bullied, blackmailed, or outright bludgeoned over the years? Was Max Schaeffer one of them? Had he pushed them too far while trying to fish for bottom feeders? They couldn't openly defy the law. They had to at least pretend to support the city's efforts to crack down on drug dealers, carjackers, and gang-bangers. But if someone like Schaeffer were to get too close to the family operation, Ricardo Tandino would feel compelled to send him a message. Which begged the question: how far would the Tandinos go? They had a reputation to protect, an image to maintain. How much room could they afford to give a cop who was just trying to do his job?

As O'Meara exited the fifth precinct parking lot, he tried to put himself in Max Schaeffer's shoes. Schaeffer was diligent, not dogged. A professional, not a perfectionist. How far would *he* go in trying to bust up the outer fringes of the Tandino network? It seemed unlikely that someone as steady as Schaeffer would exceed the mandate he had been given. His job had been to go after the lowlifes. Would he have stopped there?

O'Meara lowered the Ford sedan's driver-side visor to block the late afternoon sun, which was still burning with enough intensity to bounce heat waves off the broiling asphalt unfolding in front of him. As he slowed to a stop at a red light, a humble office front stood out among the hodgepodge of nail salons, pawnshops, and greasy spoons, and before he could talk himself out of it, he was backing into a parallel parking space out front of the Big Brothers Big Sisters office.

Inside, he was met by a redheaded receptionist with glasses so thick they shrunk her eyes to mere dots behind the lenses. "May I help you?" she asked in a crinkly voice.

"Yeah," O'Meara said, fumbling for the right way to introduce himself. "I'm with the NOPD. But I'm here on my own behalf. I want to volunteer as a big brother."

"Okay," the receptionist said. "Most of the staff has already gone home for the day. But I might be able to find someone who can help you. Can you wait just a moment?"

"Sure."

The receptionist put a call through to someone, and O'Meara took a seat on a small but cushy couch in the cramped reception area, which was separated from the rest of the office by a gray divider. Track lighting hung from the bright white ceiling and ran the length of the long and narrow space, from the reception area to the back wall. Between the reception area and the back wall were several cubicles, which no doubt served as offices, although there appeared to be little or no activity going on at the moment.

After a short interval, O'Meara was escorted to a cubicle in the back where a plump African-American woman was busily pecking away at her keyboard. Her office wasn't much—an L-shaped desk and a filing cabinet—but it was cluttered with personal touches, from a collection of African violets to several rainbow-colored crayon drawings, the latter of which had been tacked to the side of the cubicle.

Once finished with her typing, the woman closed the file she was working on and looked up at the detective, revealing a vibrant pair of eyes and a friendly, if somewhat weary, smile. "So you want to be a big brother," she said in a matronly tone while giving O'Meara the once-over.

"That's right." O'Meara tried to conjure up the priest's words from the other day. "I want to give back to the community."

"Aren't you already providing an important community service by being a member of the police force?"

"Yeah," he said. "But I want to connect with people in a less exciting way, if that makes sense."

"It does," the woman said, still clearly unconvinced. "I'll be honest with you, Officer—"

"*Detective.* It's Detective John O'Meara."

"Okay, Detective O'Meara. We get a lot of volunteers from your line of work, but not too many of them stick around. Same with firefighters. Soldiers returning from Iraq. People see awful things in the line of duty, and they come here for therapy, I guess you'd say. But, although we like to think that being a volunteer with us offers all sorts of intangible rewards, it's still about the kids, understand? If you've come to us for the wrong reasons…"

O'Meara was tempted to get up and leave. He didn't like being lumped in with a bunch of guys with PTSD. And he didn't like this woman assessing his character after knowing him all of thirty seconds. But it would take a lot more than a condescending social worker to intimidate him. "Look, I don't need therapy. You know nothing about me. I'm here to be someone's big brother. I have no criminal record, pass regular drug screening, and am a city employee. I'm the perfect candidate. You need volunteers or not?"

The woman fought off a smile. "We do, Detective. And I suppose it's possible I've misjudged you. If that's the case, I apologize."

"Apology accepted." O'Meara glanced at the woman's nametag. "So how do I get started, Cynthia Knudson? And is that a Mrs. or Ms.?"

Cynthia turned up her nose at the question. "None of your business."

"I just want to know what to call you. By the time I'm done filling out whatever paperwork you have for me, I'm sure you'll know a hell of a lot more about me than I know about you."

The scowl on her face softened. "You can just call me Cynthia."

"All right, Cynthia." She clearly had a story to tell, like most people. But O'Meara decided he'd pushed far enough for now. "What do I do to get started?"

~~~

An hour later, Detective O'Meara was striding down a short cobblestone path toward the front door to Ricardo Tandino's Garden District mansion. Unlike his nephew's gaudy Greek-columned townhouse, Ricardo's Italianate mansion was a picture of Old World style and elegance. Graceful deciduous trees and flowering shrubs softened the mansion's double-galleried exterior, framing the wrought-iron latticework with gentle hues and subtle textures. If Anthony Tandino's home had stood for unabashed virility and excess, Ricardo's was a monument to the kind of refinement and self-possession that could only come with age—and a whole lot of money.

O'Meara rang the bell, and a moment later a butler appeared. Judging by the amount of muscle that was bulging out from and over his starched collar, he could have easily passed for a tight end on the Saints' practice squad. That or a side of Grade A beef.

"May I help you?" he asked curtly.

O'Meara flashed his badge. "I need to see Mr. Tandino."

"He doesn't want to see you."

"Why don't we let him decide for himself?"

The butler said nothing, but it was clear from the

humorless expression on his face that he wasn't moved in the least to cooperate.

"It's your ass," O'Meara bluffed, "not mine. I mean, I can go get a search warrant and be back in twenty minutes, if you want. But then we'll be involving the courts, and the press will get wind of it, and things will just go south from there—all because you wouldn't grant me a couple minutes with the big guy. It's your call."

The unmovable butler failed to flinch. "You're full of shit."

O'Meara nodded coolly as he weighed his options. But the moment he spotted a smug grin beginning to form on the beefeater's face, he knew he only had one left. He whipped his gun free from his shoulder holster, pressed it against the butler's forehead, and clicked off the safety.

"All right, asshole. Take me to your boss."

"No."

"No?" O'Meara said, his voice rising. "You sure you want to play these odds? How do you know I'm not some hopped up cop ready to blow your brains out? How do you know Max Schaeffer wasn't my best friend? How do you know I'm not looking to make someone—anyone—pay for the way things went down at Tony Tandino's?"

"It's your funeral," the butler warned and with O'Meara's gun still trained at his head led the way through the entryway, past what looked like an old-fashioned Southern parlor, and down a short hallway.

After passing a couple of closed doors, they

entered the only open one, and there in the flesh was Mr. Ricardo Tandino, sleeves rolled up, his suit jacket draped over the back of a tall stool against the far wall. He had a scotch in one hand and a stogy in the other and appeared to be overseeing a game of billiards between his youngest son and some other garden-variety thug.

"I thought I told you no visitors," he said in an icy tone to the butler, ignoring O'Meara.

"Sorry, Mr. Tandino." The beefy butler nodded to the gun still trained at his head. "The guy didn't give me no choice."

"You always have a choice," Tandino said. "Life's full of choices. Right, boys?"

Neither spoke, but continued eying the detective coolly.

O'Meara recognized Louie, who was fairly short, like his father, but not nearly as stout. While the old man's silver hair was receding in front and thinning on top, Louie still had a full head of jet-black hair. He was holding a pool cue and trying to look menacing in pleated slacks and silk shirt, the latter unbuttoned to display a mess of gold chains and chest hair. When it came to his wardrobe, he certainly didn't take any cues from his father, who, even with his jacket off, was the picture of elegance in two-thirds of a dark gray three-piece suit. A bulge beneath Ricardo's silk vest revealed where he kept his gun, or at least *one* of his guns. All three were clearly packing heat. The third, a light-skinned African-American with a wild and woolly Afro and the same coke-snorting, club-going attire as Louie, had done the poorest job of camouflaging his weapon, which had been strategically hidden in his slacks to make him look better endowed than he was.

Ricardo snuffed out his cigar in a smokeless ashtray and then pointed a stubby index finger at O'Meara. "Put the gun away, Detective. And Dennis, make yourself scarce."

The butler did as he was told, clearly more afraid of his boss than the gun pointed at his head, and suddenly O'Meara was more or less alone with the most powerful man in New Orleans. He knew he shouldn't be surprised that Ricardo recognized him. The old man probably had a file on every cop in the city. But he nonetheless felt his face flush red at being identified so quickly and nonchalantly.

"How 'bout I waste him right here!" Louie said and came straight at O'Meara, barrel first. "Let me waste the fucker!"

Ricardo chuckled once and then held up his hand. "You'll have to forgive my son, Detective. We're still a little...on edge. I'm sure you understand." He waved off his lapdog and then approached O'Meara himself, and as he came to a stop only a few feet away, O'Meara got a better view of his beet-red face, the veins bulging angrily in his stout neck, and the faint scar that ran from just beneath his left eye to his jaw. "I'll admit, though: I'm a little surprised that a cop from the fifth district would have the pluck to show his face in my home. Either you've come to beg my family's forgiveness, or you're here to stir things up. Which is it?"

O'Meara cleared his throat, cognizant of Louie's friend, who had circled around to his left, no doubt angling to cut off a quick escape. "Neither, Mr. Tandino. I've come for your help."

Ricardo cocked his head slightly, the gears turning. "Louie," he said briskly, "take Sloan out back with you. I need a moment with the detective."

"You're in charge, Paps. We'll be right outside. Come on, Sloan."

Louie and his pal left through a pair of French doors that led to what from the inside looked like a small back patio and garden, each man being sure to throw one last menacing stare at O'Meara before strutting outside.

"Mr. Tandino," O'Meara said, hoping to keep the old man guessing, "I need to know everything you know about Max Schaeffer—what he was plugged into, what contacts he made in your organization."

For a split second, Ricardo Tandino looked like he might uncork an unrestrained, gut-busting laugh. But just as quickly his face darkened. "You got five seconds before I kick your can to the curb, Detective."

"Puffer fish. Do you eat the stuff, or do you just have it served to your enemies?"

"You're out of time."

"Do you extract the tetrodotoxin here, or do you have it—"

Before he could finish the sentence, O'Meara felt a blow to the back, and the next thing he knew he was being hung up like a coat on a rack, courtesy of Dennis, the butler, and one of his enormous meat hooks. But as he was being dragged out of Ricardo Tandino's aristocratic billiard room, the detective thought he caught a look of doubt in the old man's eye, and he did his best to savor that little victory, even after he landed on his ass outside the front gate.

CHAPTER 6

Detective O'Meara locked the driver's side door of the Bel Air and walked stiffly toward the stairs to his second-story apartment, stopping at the mailbox by the stairwell. His back was still throbbing from the dust-up at the Tandino mansion, as was his tailbone. He had hoped to provoke Ricardo Tandino into saying something, but the old man had lived up to his steely reputation and had revealed nothing of substance.

"Evening, Mr. O'Meara."

The detective looked up to see Edna, the sweet if somewhat eccentric spinster who lived directly beneath him. She had her white hair up in a bun and was standing in the doorway to her apartment with a basket full of laundry.

"Can I carry that to the Laundromat for you?" O'Meara asked.

"Oh, that won't be necessary, young man. It's only a few doors down. But thank you kindly."

O'Meara spied the lonely look on Edna's wrinkled face, which was weathered but still gleamed most days, and stuffed his mail into his back pocket. "Give me that," he said playfully.

She dutifully complied, handing over her basket of laundry, and O'Meara walked his neighbor and her laundry to the Laundromat, which was indeed only a few doors down from the mailbox. Three, to be exact. After loading the clothes into an empty washer for her, he left Edna to the purring chorus of machines and then limped up the stairs to his apartment. The place wasn't much—two cookie-cutter bedrooms in the blue-collar Marigny neighborhood of New Orleans—but it was all he needed.

Once inside, the detective threw his mail on the kitchen counter and then marched straight to the sliding glass door off the small dining nook. Had he been a family man, he might have kissed the wife and patted the kid (or the dog) on the head. But his routine was simpler: unfasten the shades and muscle open the sliding glass door, which had a habit of sticking on sweltering evenings like this. There was no view to speak of, unless he counted the moss growing on the backside of the neighboring building that stood less than thirty feet from his small back deck and shaded it from the hot evening sun. But there was fresh air to be had, and an apartment that had been closed up all day was sorely in need of a purifying breeze.

Though a bachelor through and through, with the mostly bare walls and sparse and Spartan furniture to prove it, the detective did like to cook. Tonight, he cracked open a beer and then stepped out onto the deck to light a few coals mounded in the bottom of an undersized grill. Dinner would be a fairly simple affair: catfish, corn on the cob, and a small bubbling pot of red beans. But he wouldn't be eating alone.

He'd barely shoveled the first bite of catfish into his mouth when his cell phone rang.

"Hey, kid," he said, picking up on the second ring.

"What's for dinner tonight?" his sister asked.

There were few things in Detective O'Meara's life that went according to plan, but an evening call from his sister could be counted on like summer rain. The two siblings were separated geographically by a thousand miles, but that didn't stop them from staying in close contact. Most brothers and sisters didn't get along as well as O'Meara and Payton did, but then most brothers and sisters hadn't lost their parents to a car accident while the eldest sibling was still in high school. From that moment on, O'Meara had taken his sister under his wing, assuming the role of protective brother, parental figure, and loyal friend. His other sister, Madeline, had already passed away, living just six years before succumbing to leukemia. Thus, after his parents' death, O'Meara's immediate family had been reduced to two: Payton and him. A kind aunt and uncle had given them a loving home in the Bronx, looking after them until each was old enough to move out. And during that time, O'Meara and Payton had become inseparable. Little had changed since then. They still spoke regularly and visited at least once a year. O'Meara often felt a psychic tether between them.

"Barbecued catfish," he answered. "How 'bout you?"

"Chinese takeout," Payton said glumly. "It's just me tonight."

"Oh yeah?" O'Meara didn't like his sister's tone, which wasn't much better than it had been the last time they talked. He tried to steer the conversation back toward the evening's menu. "Did you get the barbecued pork?"

"Uh-huh."

"Almond chicken?"

"Check."

"Fried rice?"

"Check."

O'Meara glanced down at the catfish still steaming on his plate and for a fleeting moment wished he'd ordered out. "Damn."

"It was cold by the time I got home," Payton lamented.

"That's what your microwave's for."

"I know."

"So..."

"I think Mark is having an affair."

O'Meara switched his cell phone to the other ear. He loved a lot of things about his sister, but her directness topped the list. She didn't waste time. "Why? What did he do?"

"Well, like I said the other day, he's always distracted. He's never here, even when he's here. But it's more than that. He's lost interest in...me. And last night, I swear I smelled someone else's perfume on him."

"Okay," O'Meara said cautiously. "If you have these suspicions, you'd better confront him. And the sooner the better. If it's nothing, you don't want your distrust poisoning your marriage. If it *is* something, then you need to clear the air right now—before things get too serious."

"I would," Payton said, "but he's not coming home tonight."

"What do you mean?"

"He flew out this morning for some brokers' convention in New Orleans."

O'Meara felt his jaw harden. Leaving town while his marriage was on the rocks was the perfectly cowardly thing to do—and just like Mark. "How long will he be gone? And...wait a second. Did you say New Orleans?"

"Uh-huh."

The detective's sullen frown disappeared, replaced by a Machiavellian grin. "Where's he staying?"

O'Meara spooned out the last of the red beans, stuffed his mouth with them, and gently tossed the pot and the serving spoon into the sink. An internal debate about whether to soak or get right to washing the dishes lasted all of three seconds. He filled the sink with hot water and then, after shutting off the tap, made his way to the couch, where the remote and another beer were sirens luring him to the rocks. He didn't make a habit of watching sports (he'd rather play them) or sitcoms (he'd rather live his own life) or whatever else was being featured on the local networks, but sometimes it felt good to just sit in front of the TV and meditate on nothing.

Today was one of those days. Now that he was

in charge of it, he was feeling more pressure than usual to make some headway on the Max Schaeffer case. What had begun as a simple disappearance had morphed into a murder-suicide, complete with mafia connections and exotic hallucinogens.

He frowned when a newscaster's face was the first thing to appear on the TV screen. News and Zen were like oil and water.

"Next," he said and changed channels.

Another talking head appeared.

"What is this?"

He glanced at his watch. It was eight-thirty. The evening news wasn't due to start for another—

It wasn't the Tandino name on the screen that grabbed his attention. It was the number preceding it. A newscaster was reporting live from the scene of a *second* Tandino murder. And just like that, he understood that everything he knew was now old news. Alfonso Tandino, Ricardo's oldest son and the most reclusive member of the Tandino clan, had just been gunned down at an exclusive Italian restaurant downtown. The alleged gunman had then turned the gun on himself.

O'Meara turned off the TV, grabbed his keys, and hurried for the door.

"What do we got?" he said as soon as Captain Whiting answered his cell phone.

"I don't know yet. I'm en route."

O'Meara was already backing out of his parking space, the Bel Air's huge engine rumbling gamely. "That makes two of us."

"Listen, John," the captain said hoarsely, "you've

been logging an awful lot of hours lately. We've got it covered. I'll fill you in on everything first thing tomorrow, all right? For now, get some sleep. You're going to need it."

Captain Whiting looked up from two covered corpses lying side by side, and an angry scowl appeared on his face. "I thought I told you to stay home," he said and retook his feet.

"Is that what you said?" O'Meara faked a confused look. "I thought you said to get my ass down here post haste. Bad connection, I guess."

"Right," Whiting croaked.

"How long have you been here?"

"Long enough. There's our shooter." The captain gestured to another body lying a dozen or so feet away on the restaurant's black-and-white tiled floor. It and the other bodies were laid out like spent pieces on a chessboard. "Apparently, he came in mumbling to himself and smelling like he'd just crawled out of a dumpster. The maitre d' tried to send him away, but he pushed right past him and opened up on our boys here. Neither got off a shot."

O'Meara nodded to the two bodies lying prone at Captain Whiting's feet. "And one of those is Alfonso Tandino?"

"The one and only."

Alfonso, more than any Tandino, had managed to build up a storied reputation, largely by keeping his private life extremely private. Unlike the other Tandinos, who behaved almost like celebrities, making regular public appearances with politicians and business owners and carefully cultivating their images, Alfonso kept to himself. The book on him was that he was one cool cucumber—and as cutthroat as they come. Rarely involved in the family's day-to-day operations, he thrived behind the scenes, all the while building on his mystique as the silent, ruthless son of Ricardo Tandino. Now his body was growing cold on a restaurant floor.

"What about the shooter?"

"The name is Henry Evans, according to his driver's license. No record. Not even a speeding ticket."

"Are we sure the license and the body are a match?"

"Pretty sure. He did a number on his face, but it looks similar to the one on the driver's license. From the sounds of it, as soon as he was finished with Tandino and his bodyguard, he turned his gun on himself. We've got a call out to his…"

Captain Whiting's voice trailed off, and he stiffened, his gaze stopping at the front of the dimly lit restaurant. A woman who looked to be in her late fifties or early sixties was being led by one of the officers past the yellow caution tape that restricted entry into the restaurant. Dressed conservatively in a navy-blue pantsuit, she bore a terrified expression on her round face, which was framed by graying medium-length hair.

"I got her," O'Meara said and strode toward the woman before the captain could assume the responsibility himself.

"I'm Detective John O'Meara," he said, taking her

gently by the arm and escorting her away from the bodies. "Are you Mrs. Evans?"

"Yes," she said softly. "I was told to come to the station. But I was listening to the radio on the way there, and I..." She choked back a sob. "I don't know. Something told me to come here. But...this is crazy. Henry can't be dead."

O'Meara tried to reassure her. "I hope you're right. The shooter was—"

"The *shooter*?" The blood drained from Mrs. Evans's face. "Are you saying my Henry...?"

"We don't know yet. The shooter was carrying Henry's wallet, including his driver's license. It's possible he stole it. We don't have a positive ID yet. Do you think you would be okay to...?" The detective couldn't bring himself to finish the sentence.

"Yes," she said hurriedly, nodding vigorously, her eyes wild with fear.

"All right. If you'll just follow me this way, we can—" O'Meara stopped abruptly. If Henry *was* the shooter, and if he had disfigured his face, as Captain Whiting had suggested, it was likely that he was hardly recognizable. O'Meara, remembering Max's mutilated corpse, fumbled for a way out. "Look, Mrs. Evans, normally we prefer to ID bodies at the morgue, which is why you were directed to the station. It's a more controlled atmosphere. It's private. The lighting is better. The body has been..."

"That's all right, Detective." Mrs. Evans smiled grimly. "I'm a retired nurse. I've seen a few things in my time."

"But if this is your husband—"

"This can't possibly be my husband. But even if it was, I would need to be right here doing exactly this."

"All right." O'Meara knelt down beside the body, and as he slowly peeled back the blanket covering the body, he got a whiff of what the maitre d' had complained about to Captain Whiting. The body smelled like an old long-haired dog that had spent the night outside in the rain.

"Oh my God," Mrs. Evans whispered before O'Meara was even half through removing the blanket. "That's Henry's sweater."

O'Meara, meanwhile, felt the hair on the back of his neck rise. The red soil caking the man's clothes and shoes matched the mud that had covered Max Schaeffer's tattered uniform.

He looked up at Mrs. Evans. "You sure you want to do this?"

She nodded fearfully.

"All right," he said and pulled the blanket from the remainder of the body, revealing a portly man in his mid to late fifties.

Not one but three bullet holes dotted the man's forehead. Each had made a clean entry through the front. The pool of blood on the black-and-white tiles beneath the skull hinted at messy exits. Despite such a violent death, the man's face, though showing a ghastly pallor, looked remarkably placid. Whatever had been his state of mind during his last moments, he was at peace now.

O'Meara looked up at Mrs. Evans just in time to

leap to her aid. She was in mid-swoon when he caught her and eased her onto a chair.

"Captain!" he called to Whiting, who had been standing within earshot throughout. "Can you send an EMT our way?"

The captain disappeared outside. A moment later, a stout paramedic arrived with smelling salts and a wool blanket, the latter matching the texture of his closely shorn hair and sideburns.

"I'm okay," Mrs. Evans said breathlessly and proceeded to throw up on her navy-blue pumps.

O'Meara took the blanket from the paramedic and draped it over Mrs. Evans's shoulders. "Thanks. I'll take it from here."

"This can't be!" Mrs. Evans sobbed. She hid her face in her hands and let go a long, plaintive moan. "This can't be!"

O'Meara sat down beside her and let her cry for several minutes, all the while gently rubbing her back. When she had finally composed herself, he felt safe to ask her a few questions.

"Mrs. Evans, tell me about your husband. What did he do for a living?"

"He's…he was a high school teacher," she whispered. "He taught English. Shakespeare."

"When was the last time you saw him?"

"Three days ago," she said and wiped away another round of tears. "We had a fight. A stupid fight. We do this sometimes. It never amounts to anything. He said he was going to go for a walk—you know, blow off some steam. He's done this before. Even stayed a couple nights at a hotel. He always comes back, and we always patch things up. It's my fault. I can be difficult to live with sometimes."

"But he didn't come back."

"No. I kept thinking he was just making a point and that he would come home when he was ready. I never doubted for a moment that he would come home. At least not until tonight, when the police called."

O'Meara drew his lips tightly together as he thought over his next question. "Does he own a gun?"

Mrs. Evans threw her head back indignantly. "Detective, my Henry doesn't even know how to *load* a gun, much less *fire* one. He *hates* guns. He wouldn't be caught dead with one."

CHAPTER 7

It was ten o'clock in the morning by the time Detective O'Meara poked his head into the forensics lab. Red Haugen was hunched over the portly body of Henry Evans, aging high school English teacher turned deadly gunman.

Red looked up and offered a barely detectable grin, his reddish-brown hair and freckled face glowing beneath the bright surgical lights, before resuming his communion with the dead flesh laid out at waist level. "Impeccable timing, Detective, as always."

"If that means I don't have to watch you saw into his organs or squeegee off the mess left behind," O'Meara replied, "then I thank you for the compliment."

Red straightened and paused to gently work out a kink in his back. "That means," he said, pressing his hands into his lower back and grimacing slightly, "that this gentleman has told me everything he knows."

"Which is…?"

"He and Officer Schaeffer had the same pharmacist."

O'Meara, still shaking off the lethargic aftereffects of a late night working a crime scene, tried to fire up the synapses in his brain. "Tetra whatever?"

"Tetrodotoxin, yes."

"And jimson weed?"

"*Datura stramonium.* He was also pumped full of bufotenine."

O'Meara felt the same giddy sensation he always felt when a faint line first began to appear between tangled and seemingly unrelated dots. "I suppose the only thing keeping him upright was atropine."

"You suppose correctly."

The detective remembered the red soil stuck to the bottom of Henry Evans's shoes and caked to his clothes. "What about the mud?"

"It's the same," Red answered nonchalantly.

"The same?"

O'Meara's cell phone chirped, but he quickly turned off the ringer. Red was not one to be interrupted in his work.

The toxicologist, meanwhile, ignored the disruption. "I had a conversation with Mel in the crime lab about an hour ago. She called it a match."

O'Meara felt another surge of adrenaline. "What else did she say?"

"It's definitely local." Red offered a deflating frown. "When I say local, I mean you can find it pretty much anywhere within a hundred-mile radius. There's nothing singular or telling about the soil found on our two victims. All we know is that they were likely playing in the same dirt pile."

O'Meara let his shoulders sag. "I'll take whatever I can get, Doc."

After finishing with Red, the detective checked his messages on the way to the parking lot. Cynthia Knudson from Big Brothers Big Sisters had called to let him know that he had his first appointment with Jason Edmonds, his little brother. Cynthia sounded like her usual self: protective, skeptical, and forever on the lookout for underperforming mentors. O'Meara couldn't imagine anyone better suited to the job.

———————

Even at his nephew's somber graveside service, Ricardo Tandino looked tough. He was certainly entering the twilight of his years, Detective O'Meara thought as he viewed the proceedings from a nearby grove of Southern magnolias, but the old man still carried himself like a lion. The hundred or so mourners on hand orbited around Ricardo, the father, like so many moons, and he obliged them by maintaining a stolid countenance, his eyes hidden behind aviator's sunglasses, his hands clasped in front of him.

Dressed in black and designer shades of gray, the assembly of family and close friends had gathered to pay their respects to the first victim of what had all the makings of a blood feud. This afternoon's service was ostensibly about Anthony Tandino, but last night's murder of Alfonso was still clearly a fresh wound. If the first insult had inspired shock and dismay, the second was an open invitation to war. But with whom?

In front of Anthony Tandino's above-ground crypt, a priest invoked the Psalms, staring skyward, and as the holy man cited scripture from memory, Detective O'Meara struggled to tie last night's events to Max Schaeffer's murder-suicide. In each case, an otherwise respectable and trustworthy citizen had cut down a Tandino before turning the murder weapon on himself. And in each case, the killer had been primed beforehand with an exotic neurotoxin and a handful of hallucinogens, one of which could be used to at least temporarily counter the neurotoxin's paralytic effects.

The first killer had been a cop who had drawn the unlucky assignment of infiltrating the Tandino clan. There was a connection there, O'Meara thought, even if he couldn't see it at the moment. The second killer was a harmless high school English teacher with no record. On the surface, he had absolutely zero to do with the Tandinos. Likewise, there was nothing to link him to Max Schaeffer.

Each killer had said goodbye to a loving family, a good job, and ultimately his life for the chance to kill a Tandino. Why? The drugs had clearly been undercutting each man's capacity to reason. According to the maitre d', Henry Evans had been unreachable after entering the Italian restaurant last night. Likewise, Max Schaeffer had been all but catatonic before biting down on his own pistol. Had he and Henry been blackmailed? Hypnotized? Whatever the answer, it was clear that someone else was pulling the strings. But who? The Tandino family had no shortage of enemies. Was it someone in law enforcement? Government? Was there another family intent on running New Orleans? The person or organization behind the deaths of Anthony and Alfonso had to be a formidable opponent, in any case.

The priest finished the benediction, and as the gathering began to break up, O'Meara stepped out from the shadows of the magnolias and started toward the line of limousines parked nearby. He wasn't sure what he would say to Ricardo Tandino just yet, but he figured it would come to him when he got to within speaking distance of the crime boss.

The detective had only walked a few feet when he felt himself being lifted by the back of his collar and gaining about a foot in elevation. O'Meara managed to turn himself just enough to see the man responsible for hoisting him like a flag on a pole.

Dennis, the butler with no neck and paws the size of dinner plates, smiled back at him without revealing any teeth. "He doesn't want to see you."

O'Meara felt a mixture of amusement and annoyance. "You again? You're like a broken record, you know that?"

The beefy butler didn't blink. Neither did he lower O'Meara to the ground.

O'Meara continued to crane his neck at an awkward angle, but it was no use. He wasn't going to break free, and he wasn't going to get a good look at Dennis, whose grim face was flitting in and out of view behind him in the bright afternoon sunlight. The detective, though, had no trouble seeing Ricardo Tandino's youngest son, Louie, marching straight toward him. He was flanked by Jeff Sloan and another goon.

"You got a death wish or something, cop?" Louie spat. "Put him down, Dennis."

The butler did as instructed, and O'Meara was now planted squarely on terra firma and staring down at the shorter Louie, whose olive-toned face was bristling only a few inches from his.

"Listen, fuck. My father gives everybody two strikes, capeesh? The next time you swing and miss, you're through."

"And you listen to me, Junior. If it wasn't for your friends here, you wouldn't even be—"

The meat hooks again. Along with being a snappy dresser, Dennis was an artist of sorts. He had brute strength, sure. But there was something about the way he used it. The man had finesse.

O'Meara grasped briefly and impotently at the air he was slicing through and then bounced with a thud and a groan at the foot of the magnolia he had been leaning against so inconspicuously only moments before. After a disorienting search for his center of gravity, he righted himself and glanced up at Louie and the others, who were already walking briskly toward the limousines. Dennis, the butler who should have been an Olympic shot-putter, glanced back just long enough to throw him an ornery smirk.

The detective would have smiled back, but the only thing he could do with his mouth, thanks to his throbbing backside, was grimace.

As soon as the bellhop had finished with his delivery and closed the door, Detective O'Meara flashed him his badge and then commandeered his cart.

"Official police business," the detective said.

"But—"

"Don't worry about it, kid. You'll get your cart back in a few minutes."

The gawky young man, still in his teens if the angry army of acne on his face was any indication, shrugged his shoulders and turned toward the elevators.

Not one to waste time, O'Meara pushed the squeaky cart down the hall, barging past several doors as he hurtled toward his destination: his brother-in-law's hotel room. Once outside the room, he carefully placed a finger over the peephole, knocked politely on the door with his other hand, and waited.

"Who is it?" a man's voice came after a long interval.

"Room service," O'Meara lied, doing his best to sound fifteen years younger and thirty pounds lighter.

There was a short pause, followed by a confused reply. "We didn't order dinner."

"Compliments of the house."

"What?"

"Champagne and *hors d'oeuvres.*"

The door opened partway, and Mark appeared in the gap, dressed in a white terrycloth bathrobe. "I've never heard of any hotel ever—" His eyes widened at the sight of the detective, and the annoyed look on his face disappeared, replaced by a sheet of red. "John?"

O'Meara, leaving the cart in the hallway, pushed past his duplicitous brother-in-law and into the room's cozy entryway, complete with closet and adjoining bathroom. He didn't stop until he had reached the foot of the king-size bed, where a fake-and-bake blonde wearing several layers of makeup but not a shred of clothing was sitting upright beside a pair of chrome handcuffs with the key still in them.

She instinctively grabbed a pillow to hide her gravity-defying investments and then, turning to her lover, asked in an icy tone, "Who the hell is *he*?"

"Family," O'Meara answered matter-of-factly for Mark. "The question is: who are you?" He held up a hand before she could answer. "I don't want to know. Get your things and go. Now."

She hesitated for perhaps a second and then hurriedly slid off the bed, partially covering herself with the pillow as she bounded off to the bathroom, her assets jiggling mechanically.

The detective briefly eyed the handcuffs still on the bedspread before turning to his brother-in-law, whose red-faced shame had already begun to fade.

"Look, John," Mark protested, "it's not as bad as it looks. This is just—"

"The end of your brokers' convention. You've got twenty-four hours to get your ass home and tell Payton everything. If you don't, I will."

Mark's eyes danced. "But it's not that simple, John. Telling her about this won't solve our problems. It certainly won't save our marriage."

"No," O'Meara said flatly, "but it might save my sister. Start packing."

CHAPTER 8

The sun was just going down over Lake Pontchartrain the next evening when Detective O'Meara pulled to a stop outside Ricardo Tandino's elegant mansion in the Garden District. Assuming Louie wasn't blowing smoke, O'Meara had pushed the Tandinos as far as he dared. A more cautious cop would have heeded the warning, but O'Meara, fresh off another day of investigating dead ends, was just desperate enough to continue trying his luck. Further interviews with Henry Evans's wife as well as her coworkers had yielded no new information, confirming only that, indeed, the portly high school English teacher had no relationship with the Tandinos, Max Schaeffer, or anyone else connected to the case. The guy's most egregious offense had been to return a book three days late to the New Orleans Public Library. He was a solid citizen, an exemplary one, in fact, who had somehow been transformed overnight into a cold-blooded assassin. But by whom? Who was using innocent men to take out the Tandinos? It was a question O'Meara was determined to put to Ricardo Tandino, who had to know better than anyone who his real enemies were.

The detective was almost relieved to see Dennis's chiseled face as the butler opened the door. The big guy didn't have a mouth like that brat, Louie, and what he did say he could back up with Neanderthal precision.

"He doesn't want to—"

"I know, I know," O'Meara said, interrupting the thick-necked bruiser. "Let's skip this part of the routine, Dennis, okay? Just tell Mr. Tandino I'm here and that I need to speak with him."

"No." Another artful elocution from the human wrecking ball: concise and impossible to misinterpret.

O'Meara sighed as he mulled over his options. The problem with going straight to crazy, as he had done when he had pulled his gun on the thickset butler during his last visit, was that there was nowhere to go from there—at least nowhere predictable or safe. It was tiring, sometimes, one-upping himself.

"Okay, look, Dennis. Here's what I'm going to—"

Dennis drew his semi-automatic pistol, showing uncanny speed for his size, and knocked O'Meara off his feet with a quick stiff-arm to the shoulder.

Distracted briefly by the sound of his own body sliding across the concrete front stoop, O'Meara soon heard the rumble of engines and the screech of tires out on the street. He looked up in time to see the burly butler lumbering down the walkway and straight toward two blacked-out commercial vans, each of which had just skidded to a stop out front of Tandino's mansion.

"I need backup!" Dennis hollered back toward the house and then opened up on the lead van, emptying a clip into its side panel and then another into its tires.

"Shit!" O'Meara hissed as a ragtag army of men poured out of each van and started toward Dennis and the mansion.

The first group out didn't look particularly agile, but each man was armed with an automatic weapon and enough ammo to go into business for himself.

Dennis, despite making what looked like several direct hits, was the first to go down, crumpling to his knees just as he was receiving cover fire from a handful of Tandino's men, now scurrying down the cobblestone path and engaging in what was quickly escalating into a full-blown firefight.

O'Meara, still more or less horizontal, thanks to the forearm shiver from Dennis, rolled behind a stone statue, one of two framing the front entrance, and quickly debated his options. He could lie low until the shooting died down, or join the fight. The bullets raking the courtyard told him he had a better shot at survival if he fought back. This was an all-out war, and he had just chosen sides: Ricardo Tandino's.

Staying low to the ground, he peered around the stone pedestal, sighted one of the onrushing gunmen, and squeezed off two rounds, each finding a home in the man's chest.

But the gunman, a bespectacled kid hardly out of his teens, didn't drop. He lurched backward from the initial impact, staggering briefly, and then continued forward, slower now, all the while sweeping the courtyard with what looked like an Uzi, its distinctively stubby barrel burping fire.

O'Meara squeezed off two more rounds, once again aiming at and hitting the bespectacled gunman in the center of his chest.

This time, the kid fell to his knees, but he kept on firing. Hardly able to hold himself up, he no longer bothered to aim his rifle or look for targets. After he had shot up the kneecaps of two of his own men, a towering, broad-shouldered man appeared out of nowhere, his dark-skinned face and body hardly more than an inky silhouette in the fading twilight, and dispatched the young man with a quick burst of bullets to the skull.

O'Meara felt a familiar sensation run the length of his spine.

Who the hell is that?

Although the detective could barely make him out in the darkening gloom, it was obvious by the way the man moved—fearlessly and deliberately, like a predator—that he was the person in charge of this massacre. And this *was* a massacre. Dennis and a few of Tandino's men had gone down, but most of those lying motionless on the ground belonged to the intruders, who, despite outnumbering the Tandinos two to one, moved with something just shy of indifference, like sleepwalkers, trancelike and impervious to the rounds whistling through their ranks. None wore bulletproof vests or any kind of body armor that O'Meara could detect, yet they went down only after sustaining multiple lethal hits. Were they hopped up on something? The one exception was the mystery man now towering over the dead body at his feet. He had knifed through the darkness like a big cat: wild *and* sober, daring *and* wily.

After offing his own man, he spied Dennis, who was crawling toward the relative safety of a stone fountain nearby, and leapt lustily after the gravely wounded butler.

O'Meara, his heart pounding in his ears, took aim at the strange man and fired three times.

Rather than recoil in pain, the man straightened angrily and searched for his shooter. And for the first time since O'Meara had spotted him, a hint of hesitation showed in the man's body language as he surveyed the carnage around him. His army, though intrepid, couldn't match Tandino's men in speed or dexterity. Soon he would be the last attacker standing.

Seemingly impervious to bullets, he wasn't beyond the reach of reason. He had begun a stealthy retreat when he caught sight of something that froze him where he stood. O'Meara followed the shadowy man's gaze to the front door, where none other than the father himself stood, AK47 blazing at his hip. Unable to resist a free shot at Ricardo Tandino, the man unloosed a hail of bullets at the front porch, and just like that, without drama or fanfare, the old man went down hard and disappeared from view.

A split second later, the mysterious man was leaping into the lead van and leaving his comrades for dead, the punctured tires on his getaway vehicle warbling sickly as he jumped on the gas.

O'Meara bolted for the front gate, zigzagging as he ran, although few of the attackers remained upright, much less standing, to prevent his escape. One last look back at the hazy chaos engulfing Ricardo Tandino's mansion told him he would be the only one giving chase.

The blacked-out van, meanwhile, came back to him in less than three blocks. It was a wounded duck, incapable of eluding anyone, let alone O'Meara in his unmarked Ford sedan, which could run down anything that drove on four wheels. But much to the detective's chagrin, the van wouldn't need to outrun him. It was hobbling straight toward the French Quarter.

CHAPTER 9

This wasn't the first time Detective O'Meara had chased a fleeing suspect into a crowd. But this man, a giddy shadow dancing through the throngs of people choking Bourbon Street, fled without fear or urgency. A head taller than most of the people in his way and the owner of a rangy frame, he nevertheless shimmied through the swarms of tourists and nighttime revelers like a cheetah rocketing through a herd of slow-moving elephants. He had ditched his staggering, clattering van two blocks earlier, and now, wheeling down the sidewalk on his own two feet, he was clearly toying with the detective, slowing down every now and then to let O'Meara steal a glimpse of the wild look in his eyes, of the sweat glistening on his midnight-black skin.

While still in the sedan, O'Meara had called in the chase to the dispatcher, but there was no telling when—or *if*—backup would arrive. He had run down enough thugs to know that the point man, the officer making first contact, often carried the full burden of capturing and cuffing the suspect.

Bourbon Street, meanwhile, formed a perfect gauntlet with its overhanging balconies, overflowing bars, and overabundance of wandering, eyes-to-the-sky tourists, each one a potentially chase-ending speed bump. O'Meara and the ghostly man rumbling down the street ahead of him were perfectly boxed in on all sides, with nowhere to go but deeper into the tangle of people.

The man's broad back was a tempting target, as were his churning feet, probably pushing size fifteen, which barely skimmed the ground between strides. How hard would he be to take down? One bullet, delivered to the lower extremities, would be enough to send him sprawling. It would also be enough to get O'Meara in hot water. Gunplay here, amidst so many people, was professional suicide. The detective's only hope was a misstep or a miscalculation. But the suspect, dressed head to toe in black, from his wool cap to his leather topsiders, didn't seem the type to make either.

As soon as O'Meara had ruled out the possibility of ending this race with a well-placed bullet, the suspect produced a handgun of his own, fishing it free from beneath his black T-shirt without breaking stride. He turned just long enough to throw a devilish smile at the detective and then began waving it wildly at the horrified pedestrians in his path.

Would he shoot? Or was he just torturing the gaping-mouthed tourists?

To hell with it! O'Meara thought and reached for his gun. He couldn't afford to wait for an answer.

The next few seconds—each one the equivalent of hours or even days spent doing nothing—slowed to a surreal stutter.

O'Meara jerked to a full-stop.

Widened his stance.

And pumped three rounds into the fleeing phantom's back.

And the suspect kept on running, his baritone laughter echoing long after he had disappeared into the night.

Chapter 10

Captain Whiting slammed shut the door to his office and then plunked down behind his desk. "All right," he said hoarsely, "let's go through this mess one more time."

"But Jim, I already—"

"You already filed a report. I know. And we went through all this last night. But that was before I had the chief of police and the mayor breathing down my neck. What the hell were you thinking, getting yourself caught up in a Western-style shootout in the French Quarter? On Bourbon Street, for Christ's sake!"

Detective O'Meara felt like a kid in the principal's office. He had no choice but to answer the captain's questions. "It wasn't a shootout," he said, rubbing the sleep out of his eyes. "He never fired a shot."

"Exactly. So you decided to discharge your weapon in a neighborhood where there are more tourists per square foot than cockroaches!" Whiting let go an angry huff masquerading as a sigh. "Let's start from the beginning. Tell me again: why did you go to the Tandinos?"

O'Meara, calling on what remained of his patience, humored the captain one more time. "I was hoping to talk to Ricardo Tandino."

"Why?"

"Both Max Schaeffer and Henry Evans were model citizens before they shot up the Tandinos. Their autopsies revealed they were on identical drugs."

"Tetrodotoxin," Whiting chimed in.

"Plus several hallucinogens. It's possible that someone is using innocent people to take out the Tandinos one at a time."

"How?"

"The person pulling the strings pumps the victim full of drugs and then sends them out to do a job."

"But even on drugs, why would the person comply?"

"I don't know. Blackmail. Hypnosis, maybe."

Captain Whiting paused a moment, massaging his bald forehead with his right hand as he mulled over the detective's answers. "So why go to Tandino?"

"I figured he would know better than anybody who his real enemies are."

"Okay. So you're there all of five seconds and two blacked-out vans pull up and start shooting up the place."

"Right."

"Do you think these men in the vans were on the same drugs as Schaeffer and our English teacher?"

"Maybe. They were definitely on something."

"Did they fire the first shot?"

O'Meara frowned. "Actually, no. One of Tandino's men fired first. He saw them coming and knew exactly what was about to go down. He was the first to get hit."

"So there were injuries? How many?"

"I don't know. Several."

"Any fatalities?"

O'Meara recalled the bodies littered across Tandino's front courtyard. "Undoubtedly."

"Well, see, that's where we get conflicting accounts. We can't get anyone past Tandino's front gate, of course, since he's got his lawyers working overtime, not to mention the fact that he owns half the judges in this parish. But he's claiming no one was hurt and—get this—that last night's racket was a simple weapons malfunction."

O'Meara did a double-take. "He's alive?"

"Why wouldn't he be?"

"I saw him go down."

"Well, if he went down, he's back up." The captain, clearly trying to maintain a line of questioning, closed his eyes a moment to regain his focus. "Did you get a good look at any of the rifles Tandino's men were firing?"

"You're hoping they're illegal."

Captain Whiting nodded.

"No," O'Meara said resignedly. "I was looking more at the people firing at me. I can tell you nothing *they* were using was legal. Not at shooting ranges, and definitely not within city limits."

The captain unfurled a tired frown. "Last night, you called it a 'war.' And that's what neighbors are calling it, too. We got stray bullets as far as four blocks away. The Tandinos won't be able to keep the courts—or the press—at bay for long. Even *they* can't cover up something like this. People are demanding straight answers. But if we can't produce bodies or even evidence of injury…"

"What about the hospitals?" O'Meara asked. "Has anyone checked with Charity?"

"We've called all the hospitals. Nobody matching the description of your suspect was admitted last night, and there were no gun-related injuries reported anywhere."

"Okay. What about the vans? When I left the Tandino residence, there was still one parked out front. Then there was the one that the suspect left in the middle of the street when he ditched it and fled on foot."

"Impounded. Both were reported stolen last week."

"No trail, in other words."

"No trail."

O'Meara shrugged and stood up. "I guess I've got my work cut out for me."

The captain pointed with his eyes to the chair. "We're not through yet."

"Oh," O'Meara said and sank back into his chair. "All right. Hit me."

"We've combed the balconies and storefronts near where you say you fired at the suspect. There's nothing there. No bullet holes. No damage."

O'Meara felt a surge of vindication. "I told you: I didn't miss once."

"But you still fired on a suspect in a crowd!" Captain Whiting croaked.

"He drew his weapon and was waving it at bystanders. I had no choice."

"You're probably right," Whiting said with a sigh. "But I can't let you off with just a scolding. The mayor wants the department to conduct an official review."

"Then do it," O'Meara said and stood up once again. "I've got nothing to hide."

The detective was pulling into Charity Hospital when his cell phone chirped.

"O'Meara," he said, not bothering to hide the agitation in his voice.

"Detective, this is Cynthia."

O'Meara suffered a brief moment of foggy uncertainty as he tried to jar his memory. *Cynthia?* And then he felt the twin pangs of recognition and remorse. It was Cynthia from Big Brothers Big Sisters. He had forgotten his appointment with Jason last night.

"Cynthia, I don't know what to say."

"You can start by admitting that you don't have time to be a big brother," she said coolly.

O'Meara got out of his car and locked the door. "Nope. Sorry. I'm not going to make it that easy for either of us. I want another shot."

"Detective, in case you didn't know, the young men and women enrolled in our program are desperate for meaningful connections with dependable adults. You missing your first appointment sets an awful precedent. You left that boy hanging."

"I was chasing a suspect on foot after getting shot at by a bunch of drugged-out crazies. I think he'll understand."

"I wouldn't count on it."

O'Meara paused outside the automatic doors at the hospital entrance. "Give me another shot. I won't let you down."

"It's not me I'm worried about," Cynthia harrumphed. "It's the boy."

"I won't let him down, either," O'Meara said. "You have my word."

"Oh, brother," Cynthia said in a low tone. "I hope I'm wrong about you, Detective. I sincerely do."

The detective chuckled wryly and then, after rescheduling a time for his first appointment with Jason, said goodbye. He then stepped into the air-conditioned comfort of the rundown hospital and followed signs to the ER, where he found Dr. Emily Stowe, a graying woman in her midfifties, scribbling something onto a clipboard at the front desk.

As the place that saw most of the city's hard-luck cases, from homeless junkies to penniless and undocumented domestic workers, Charity Hospital provided an unvarnished glimpse of the underside of New Orleans. According to Captain Whiting, phone calls had already been made to all the area's hospitals, including Charity, with no luck. But there was always the possibility that the suspect, growing increasingly desperate (and low on blood), had checked himself in within the last hour or so. Moreover, O'Meara knew that sometimes a face-to-face visit yielded more information than a mere phone call. Regardless, no visit was a waste of time. Maintaining ongoing relationships with people in the community paid dividends down the line.

"Excuse me," O'Meara said. "Who do I talk to about getting my prostate examined?"

Dr. Stowe looked up and crinkled her nose at the detective. "It's always a pleasure, Detective O'Meara," she said, lowering her clipboard. "What can I do for you?"

A slim, attractive woman, she was mostly obscured by the long front desk, behind which doctors and physicians' assistants regularly wrote prescriptions and filled out charts. Behind her, thousands of patient files, stacked vertically in endless rows with the shelves running floor-to-ceiling, competed for space. The lighting, like the rest of the hospital, was sterile, if somewhat bleak. Although clean, the tile floor had seen better days and was severely scuffed from years of abuse.

"Just curious if anybody's been through with a gunshot wound in the last twelve hours or so," O'Meara said.

"Are the bullets yours?" the doctor asked with raised eyebrows.

O'Meara nodded.

"Well, I hate to disappoint you, but it's been awfully quiet around here. Nothing this morning. And from the sounds of it, nothing last night."

"Nothing?"

"We've had three overdoses, one hit-and-run victim, two accidental stabbings, and the usual potpourri of sick kids and overwrought hypochondriacs. But no gunshot victims."

O'Meara was genuinely surprised. New Orleans owned the highest murder rate of any big city in the U.S., and much of it was due to gun violence. "That's got to be some kind of record."

Dr. Stowe removed her reading glasses and slipped them into the breast pocket of her white overcoat. "Believe it or not, we sometimes go days between gunshot wounds. Then we get hit with several cases at once."

"Too bad you can't spread 'em out a little more evenly."

The good doctor shrugged. "Yeah, well, life's a lot of things, Detective, but it ain't neat and tidy. So," she said, throwing O'Meara a mischievous smile, "how *is* your prostate, anyway?"

———

Ricardo Tandino snuffed out what was left of his cigar in a smokeless ashtray and then fixed his gaze on Doc Vizzini, who was washing his hands in the sink behind the bar. Mario "Doc" Vizzini was no older than Ricardo, but with his back hunched over the sink and his bespectacled eyes cast downward, he looked like someone with one foot in the grave. Like Ricardo, the doctor was a second-generation American with Italian roots that ran deep. And like Ricardo, he wasn't getting any younger.

"It's been awhile since we pulled an all-nighter, Doc. How you holding up?"

Doc looked up from the sink and turned toward

Ricardo, revealing a bloodshot pair of eyes. "I doubt I have too many of these left in me, old friend."

"Me neither. So...what do you think? Is he gonna make it?"

Doc gestured toward Ricardo's arm, which was still throbbing but resting snugly in a sling. "I wish I could patch him up as neatly as I did you. But he got shot up pretty bad."

Dennis had been the first of Ricardo's men to go down in the fighting the night before, and, assuming recovery was still a possibility, he would be the last among the living to retake his feet. A total of nine men, including Ricardo himself, had been hit. Three were already mobile, two were sitting upright, and one, Dennis, was hanging on for dear life in the guestroom down the hall. The other three were dead—and had arrived that way at Doc Vizzini's makeshift OR in the billiard room. With the help of Ricardo's unhurt men, Doc had set up a triage on one side of the room and an operating theater on the other, with one of the pool tables serving as the operating table.

Ricardo pointed a stubby finger at the blood-soaked table. "You did good work, Doc, like always. But next time, try to take it easy on the furniture. That belonged to my grandfather. Cost a fortune to have it shipped here from the Old Country."

"I'll do that if you tell my patients to stop bleeding."

Ricardo laughed once and then winced. Movement of any kind sent pain radiating from his right bicep, through which two rounds had passed cleanly.

"Why don't you let me give you something for that

arm?" Doc said and then lifted his glasses to get at his eyes, rubbing them tiredly.

"No thanks, Doc. I gotta have my wits about me while I clean up this mess."

Mess, of course, was an understatement. There were high-priced attorneys to placate, nosy media types to ward off, and the police to stall. Then there was the matter of finding out who the hell was waging war on the Tandino family. Louie and Sloan had taken the roughly seventeen bodies of their attackers, some of which had been hastily reassembled, their remains scooped into plastic bags, and ferried them to an associate's meat-packing warehouse, where they were now on ice, awaiting proper identification and post-mortem investigation. It was likely the boys had been tailed by the police, but Ricardo was hopeful he could have the bodies examined and turned into sausage before a court order was granted to investigate the warehouse. Ideally, he would have liked to have gotten his hands on at least one of the vans belonging to the attackers, but the vans had nevertheless served a useful purpose. In impounding them, the police had been forced to expend some of their resources on something other than peering over the wrought-iron fence while trying to gather evidence of the previous night's slaughter.

Ricardo heard footsteps on the back patio and turned in time to see Louie and Sloan enter through the French doors. The two boys, having already combed the front, had been out back collecting spent shells and other evidence of the firefight.

"Find anything interesting?" Ricardo asked gruffly.

He was still peeved at his youngest son, who had fired on the intruders from the safety of the house, thereby inviting plenty of property-damaging return fire in the process. When it came to material possessions, and Ricardo had assembled more than his fair share, there was nothing that he valued more than his home, a tangible, visible expression of his success as well as his longevity.

"No," Louie said glumly, "but there's something we need to talk about."

Ricardo felt his blood simmer. His son's tone indicated that a mistake of some kind had been made, that an apology was in the offing. "Doc," he said, turning to his long-time friend, "why don't you go see how Dennis is doing."

Doc removed his bloody apron and tossed it into a nearby garbage can on his way out. "Will do."

Ricardo motioned to the French doors the boys had just walked through. "Sloan, I'd like you to take another look while Louie and I talk."

Louie's best friend nodded and made a quick exit, leaving just Ricardo and his youngest son in the billiard room.

Ricardo turned to the boy. "All right. Let's hear it."

Louie, dressed as always in a silk shirt and tight-fitting slacks, glanced away nervously. "It's like this, sir. You remember a lowlife by the name of Papa G?"

Ricardo lit another cigar and straddled one of the barstools, trying in vain to conjure up a face to go with the name. "Barely," he said after tiring of the exercise. "He was just an amateur if I remember correctly—

someone trying to muscle in on our territory. But he talked like he thought he should be crowned the goddamned King of New Orleans."

"That's him!" Louie said anxiously.

"Well, what about him? You boys took care of him years ago."

"Yes!" Louie answered, his nasally voice unleashing a torrent of nervous energy. "We tossed him from a fifth-story window near the canal. Shot him up on his way down. I even ran over him a couple times for good measure. He was deader than anything you see on the side of the highway."

Ricardo didn't like the uncertainty in his son's voice. "So?"

"Well, see, all of us saw him there. He was dead. And that was the end of him. We did such a good job on him that we didn't have to worry for years about dealers trying to carve out a piece of our pie. We made an *example* of him, and everybody took note, see?"

"So what's the problem?" Ricardo asked, not bothering to hide the annoyance in his voice.

Louie laughed nervously. "You're not gonna believe this. *We* hardly believe it. But Sloan and I both got a pretty good look at the guy that winged you last night, and we're pretty sure it was that crazy son of a bitch, Papa G."

Ricardo stood up, deposited his cigar in the smokeless ashtray next to him, and strode toward his son, stopping just a few feet from his face, close enough to see the nervous speckles of saliva on the kid's mouth. "*How* sure?"

CHAPTER 11

"Grace," Papa G said tiredly, "help me into this thing."

His attendant, dressed in a white denim halter top and matching micro-skirt, motioned to the other two scantily clad women lingering near the doorway to Papa G's spacious bathroom, and the three lovelies lowered their benefactor into the bath, the big man grimacing as his raw but already healing flesh made contact with the soapy water.

Papa G let loose a guttural utterance, half groan, half blue streak, and then closed his eyes to the pain. Immortality, if that was indeed what he had achieved, had not come without a price. Last night's raid at the Tandino estate, followed by the wild romp down Bourbon Street, had earned him a legion of welts and bruises, each one a palpable sign of the crossover from human to something else. He thought back to the day Louie and Sloan had thrown him from a fifth-story window. He was stronger now, more tapped into his power. And he was more willing than ever to endure suffering if it meant sowing fear and doubt in the hearts of his enemies.

But what exactly was he? A god? Some kind of super villain? He wasn't sure.

What he did know—and he could feel it in his wounds—was that part of him, at least, was still human. He could still ache. His skin could still recoil from stabbing pain. And he still warmed to the soothing touch of a woman.

"Shoulders," he whispered to Grace.

His lover, needing no more instruction, dutifully went to work on his neck and shoulders, each finger doling out a healing balm of comfort and warmth. It wasn't just his relationship with bullets that had changed, Papa G realized. Caresses, too, felt different on his skin, which, if it was largely immune to mortal hazards, was inversely alive to physical pleasure.

"Last night was crazy," Grace cooed. Her voice felt like a spring breeze on his skin. "You need to be more careful."

"What do you know?" he asked, uninterested in an answer.

She said nothing as her hands migrated from his shoulders to his chest, each one tracing a path over his heart.

Ten years ago, he had fallen five stories to his death. His nascent powers, dumb and unrealized at the time, had since grown in depth and breadth. He knew more. Intuited more. *Saw* more. He could see everything, including the future. He saw water rising. Levees crumbling. He saw a city submerged. He saw old people left to drown in their living rooms, while other hardier souls hacked their way out of their attics to escape an infernal heat. He saw hordes of cockroaches and snakes clinging to anything that would float, clouds of mosquitoes blooming in the hazy night sky, an oily brown sludge rising to the floodwater's surface. He saw women raped on rooftops and looters defecating in cash registers. He saw the end of days, a fetid, bloated apocalypse, and knew it was coming for New Orleans.

"Grace," he said without opening his eyes, "get in here with me."

Detective O'Meara stepped inside Franny's Pet Palace and wrinkled his nose at the pungent odors that hung in the stale air. He hadn't bugged Lenny Pointer in a few days, and as he made his way to the fish aisle where the former convict always lurked, he pondered how best to approach him. Lenny responded to intimidation on occasion, but typically the best way to tweeze information from him was to gently extract it, one piece at a time. The guy was most helpful, though, when it suited him. If he was in a friendly or talkative mood when the detective found him, if he was floating on an even keel, the exchange would invariably produce, if not a useful bit of information, at least a general atmosphere of pliability and cooperativeness. Lenny would still act nervous, of course, suffering through the encounter in all his twitchy glory. But he would give the impression that he and the detective were on the same team. If he was feeling sullen or put upon, on the other hand, he would impart nothing but negative vibes. The latter, unfortunately, had been his knee-jerk response of late. Since Max Schaeffer's disappearance, Lenny, like the rest of the neighborhood, had been on a knife's edge.

Last night's shootout had gone down in the Garden District, while the surreal chase of the phantom man had been confined to Bourbon Street and the French Quarter. But surely news of both events had found its way to the Lower Nine. How were residents here reacting to the latest developments in the war between the Tandinos and their mysterious enemy? More importantly, did anyone know the identity of the man O'Meara had shot last night? Was he holed up somewhere nearby, nursing his wounds? If the suspect had even a tenuous connection to the neighborhood, Lenny would know what that connection was.

The detective turned the corner and was surprised to find an empty fish aisle. Other than the push broom resting upright against one of the empty tanks, there was no evidence of Lenny. O'Meara looked at his watch. It was well past lunchtime. Was Lenny on a break? In the bathroom, maybe? Had he called in sick?

O'Meara returned the way he had come and stopped at the checkout counter, where Franny herself was busily tagging several chew toys. In her early sixties, with a head too big for her tiny frame, she was only rarely seen in the store that bore her name. Usually Lenny and one or two high school kids kept the place running.

She looked up from her work and frowned when she recognized the detective. "He ain't here," she said, anticipating O'Meara's question.

"Is he sick?"

"Dunno."

"You don't know?"

"That's what I said," she drawled lazily. Wearing huge hoop earrings, far too much ruby-red lipstick, and fake eyelashes—but dressed in a frumpy beige dress that could have passed for a gunnysack—Franny cut the figure of someone who did whatever the hell she wanted. She had run her business in the same location for the better part of three decades and was as much a part of the landscape as the shotgun shacks that littered the Ninth Ward.

"Didn't he call in?"

"Nope." She didn't sound disappointed so much as vindicated. She had always maintained that employing a former convict could only lead to trouble, and now she had proof. Why she had taken on Lenny in the first place spoke to the other half of her personality, which clearly relished projects of the human variety.

O'Meara nodded guardedly. He wasn't quite ready to sound the alarm bell. But his sick sense told him there was more to this than just a simple misunderstanding or oversight on Lenny's behalf. Lenny had been sober every day since he had been released from prison, and his job here had played a large part in that. He was either feeling so lousy he couldn't get to the phone or was in serious trouble. O'Meara, though pessimistic, hoped it was something trivial, like food poisoning or viral pneumonia.

O'Meara shifted in his chaise longue, and the back of his legs stuck momentarily to the soft, rubbery rungs. The air-conditioning unit in his apartment had croaked the night before, which meant that it was better to endure the evening out here, on his back deck with a view of the backside of the next building, than to languish inside. It was too hot to cook. Too hot, even, to barbecue. He would sip a beer and pick at a plate of cold beans instead.

The heat, of course, wasn't nearly as bad as the humidity that came with it. The two were part of a package deal, unfortunately, and in New Orleans, it seemed residents rarely experienced one without the other. Hurricane season brought with it a perverse hope for an end to the torturously hot lull, a way out of the stagnant heat, even if that meant riding out a hurricane in the process. Landfall almost always occurred somewhere else on the coast, either east or west of New Orleans proper, and the city, after breathing a sigh of relief that it had once again been spared the worst ravages of the latest storm, invariably awoke to cleaner, cooler skies, indeed, to a different world made anew by Mother Nature. One night of fingernail-biting, accompanied by high winds and heavy rains but no real damage, seemed a fair tradeoff for the almost eerie tranquility that followed.

But it was still fairly early in the season. No hurricane had yet to put New Orleans in her crosshairs. Which meant the sticky, stifling days and nights would march on for the time being, with no end in sight.

O'Meara's cell phone punctured the lazy silence. "Hey, sis," he said, not waiting for a second ring. "How're you doing?"

"Hanging in there," she said in a resolute tone. It

was obvious she had been crying, which meant her husband had indeed flown back to New York and come clean about his infidelity.

"I take it you talked to Mark."

"I did. He said you walked in on quite a scene at the hotel. He also said you wouldn't leave until he packed his bag and made a reservation for the first flight home. Said you insisted that he be honest with me about *everything.*"

"Well, it was the least—"

"He's leaving."

O'Meara's eyes widened. He had envisioned several potential scenarios, including the one he had thought was most likely, which was that Payton would scold Mark for cheating on her and then, after a long, hard struggle, forgive him and take him back into her heart. It had never dawned on him that her spineless husband would use the occasion to end their marriage.

"I don't know what to say, Payton."

"Me, either," she said between sniffles.

"What are you going to do?"

"Give him what he wants."

"A divorce?"

"Yeah."

O'Meara sat quietly, unsure what to say.

"It's for the best," Payton said in a sober voice. "From the sounds of it, he fell out of love pretty much the second I said, 'I do.' You know Mark—he's *so* competitive. It's all about the challenge for him. I was just another deal to make, another mountain to conquer. Once he had me, he was looking for the next adventure. I could have never kept him happy."

"No one could," O'Meara shot back. "I'll be honest, Payton: I never liked the guy. He's a shark. I mean, he's a good-looking guy. He's successful and all. But he's got wandering eyes, you know? He's a player."

"A shark, a player," Payton said bitterly. "I guess I knew all that. But I thought I could change him. I thought maybe…" Her voice trailed off, replaced by a quiet sob. "I guess I thought he just needed to be loved."

If O'Meara had played the role of the great protector in their youth, Payton had been the caretaker. Every stray cat, lost dog, and friendless schoolmate had at some point ended up in her care. Despite the fact that she had lost her parents, she had always exhibited a selfless streak, a seemingly bottomless capacity to look after those around her. It was no surprise to the detective that she had viewed her husband in such a way. He was just another loser needing saving. O'Meara suddenly wished he had clocked the guy while he'd been in the same hotel room with him. But he also felt relief that Mark would no longer be able to hurt his sister. She would grieve the end of their marriage, certainly. Payton, never one to bottle up her feelings, wore her heart on her sleeve. But she would get over him. She was sweet—but tough as nails.

"What can I do, kid?"

She laughed softly into the phone. "Just keep being my big brother."

CHAPTER 12

Forty-eight hours after the shootout at the Tandino estate, Detective O'Meara brought the Bel Air to a stop beside a rundown park. It didn't amount to much: two abandoned basketball courts, a metal slide so hot no one dared touch it with bare skin, even now, at six o'clock in the evening, and a sandpit inhabited only by the stump of a teeter-totter, long since hauled away. A decrepit bench, decorated with pigeon droppings and leaning due south, sat beneath a lone elm tree, the park's only source of shade. Everything, including the tree's broad and gnarled trunk, was layered with graffiti.

Lacing up his shoes on the blacktop beneath one of the net-less basketball hoops was an African-American kid, fifteen and a half years old, with dark brown skin and a closely shorn Afro. A bright orange basketball, brand new by the looks of it, sat idle beside him.

"You must be Jason," O'Meara said.

The kid stood up and offered a firm handshake.

"That's me," he said, assuming the cool calm of someone who had seen and done it all already. "You missed the orientation, man."

The two were supposed to have met an hour earlier with Cynthia Knudson at the Big Brothers Big Sisters office. But work had run long, as usual. O'Meara, despite already treading on thin ice with Cynthia, had called her while Jason had been sitting beside her in her cubicle and convinced her to let the two meet here after hours. She had left the decision up to Jason, and he had consented without hesitation.

Jason Edmonds, though long and lean and an inch or so taller than the detective, looked every bit his young age, thanks to his smooth, wrinkle-free hands, pearly white teeth, and what could only be called a baby-face.

"I appreciate your flexibility," O'Meara said. "My job sometimes keeps me late."

The kid gave him an appraising look. "You're a cop, right?"

O'Meara nodded. "I'm a detective with the fifth district. Narcotics."

"You must see all sorts of crazy shit."

"I do," O'Meara said with a chuckle.

Jason scooped up the ball and motioned to the rim hanging over them. "So you any good?"

"I'm all right," O'Meara answered, "for an old white guy with no hops."

A toothy grin appeared on Jason's face. "Maybe I can teach you a thing or two."

"Maybe."

And with that, keys, watches, and anything that

could inhibit their movement were removed and placed next to the detective's duffel bag, out of bounds and out of the way. Half-court basketball, played in the day's waning heat with the evening sun as backdrop, had seemed to O'Meara the perfect way to melt the ice with Jason, which was why he had suggested it. The fact that Jason had agreed so readily to the pickup game was proof that most every inner city kid, whether in New Orleans or the Bronx, understood the language of street basketball, which was equal parts finesse and brute force, chivalry and treachery.

It rarely took more than a few minutes, a few trips up and down the shortened court, to gauge the caliber of an opponent, and O'Meara quickly sussed out Jason's strengths and weaknesses. He had a long wingspan and deftly used his lanky features to his advantage. He wasn't terribly strong, but he was quick and had good instincts. After the kid swatted away a fade-away jumper for his second straight block, O'Meara understood there were certain shots that just weren't going to fly against him. The detective's laziest habits on the court, like floating off his weak foot or hanging in the air too long before releasing the ball, would earn him nothing but scorn and humiliation. He would have to earn every point, because every jumper, every drive would be contested. In other words, this was going to be hard work.

After forty-five minutes of sweating and grunting, the detective had had enough. "Let's take a break," he said between pants.

"Sure," Jason said, his dark brown skin barely showing the first glint of perspiration.

"You sure you're only a sophomore?" O'Meara said, lowering himself to the warm asphalt and digging into his duffel bag for his water bottle.

"I will be next month when school starts."

"You trying out for the school team?"

"I guess so," Jason said with a disinterested shrug.

"You *guess* so?"

Another shrug.

O'Meara had seen it before: nonchalance masking fear. Whether Jason feared failure or success or both, it was clear he didn't feel particularly safe sticking his neck out in front of his peers. Making the school team, especially the varsity squad, would give him serious credentials. But getting cut would dash more than his ego. According to Cynthia, Jason's father had died of a heart attack while the kid had still been in diapers. He'd been raised ever since by his widowed mother, although in truth, his grandmother, a colorful character by all accounts, had done much of the parenting, since Mrs. Edmonds toiled long hours on an assembly line. The kid had no male role models to speak of and, whether or not the two were related, came off as overly cautious to those around him. He was warm and down to earth, thanks to the influence of his mother and grandmother. But he lacked the confidence needed to realize his full potential.

That was where the detective came in. His job would be to give the kid a little buoyancy, a little…

Hell, O'Meara thought, who was he kidding? If anybody needed a confidence booster, it was the thirty-six-year-old white guy sprawled on the pavement and gasping for air.

A couple of hours later, O'Meara was recuperating at his favorite neighborhood watering hole, an old-fashioned English pub that served beefy, weighty burgers and beer so stout it could be quaffed in place of a meal. O'Meara, taking a seat at the bar, planned to enjoy both.

The pub was owned and run by Jack Murray, who tended bar most nights. An older gent with a leathery face and a pair of forearms like Popeye's, he was as much a fixture as the creaky old planks beneath his feet and the dark wood paneling that gave his place its dusty charm. As soon as he had finished with a customer, he made his way over to O'Meara. "You look like you just climbed Mt. Everest, Detective."

"I feel like it, too," O'Meara replied. "Just got my ass dragged all over a basketball court by a fifteen-year-old kid."

Jack laughed from his belly. "You want the usual?"

Too tired to say another word, O'Meara merely nodded, and seconds later, he was staring down at a Dixie with a Spanish accent, otherwise known as a pint of beer with olives on the side. If tonight unfolded like most nights here, he would just be draining the last of his beer when Jack arrived with his hamburger and fries.

The last two days had unfolded in an equally predictable fashion. Captain Whiting had treated him with kid gloves while the rest of his colleagues at the precinct had given him a wide berth—par for the course while the subject of an official review. No one wanted to trample on his feelings, or, for that matter, be associated with him in any way. The review, of course, would come to nothing. But it had to be conducted, lest the mayor fret that the captain, and by extension the city, had no control over its police force. Shooting at bad guys, if doing so had the potential to take away tourist dollars, had to be roundly condemned.

The investigation of the Tandinos, meanwhile, had gone nowhere. Although Ricardo had built a reputation as a tough guy, he was, with the help of his high-priced attorneys, as smooth as an oil slick. He had successfully deflected, stalled, or complicated every effort by the police to examine the evidence left in the wake of the firefight at his estate. As a result, O'Meara had viewed in real time far more than he or any of his fellow detectives had managed to dig up in the battle's aftermath. He had no eyewitnesses, other than himself, no bodies, and no legal avenues available to him. All he could do was continue circling—and bide his time.

What stuck with the detective most from that night, however, had nothing to do with the smoking carnage out front of Tandino's Italianate mansion. It was the memory of the mysterious suspect that haunted him. There had been something about the man that was uncanny. Almost...unearthly. Although clearly flesh and blood, he had nevertheless struck O'Meara as somehow above the fray, like a puppet master among dummies, royalty among beggars. He had dispatched one of his own men without hesitation or remorse, knocked Ricardo Tandino off his feet with one sweep of his rifle, and then rumbled down Bourbon Street with wild, grinning eyes. While horrified tourists had parted before him like an ever-widening sea, he had kept the detective at a safe but tantalizingly close distance, toying with him, provoking him. And instead of arching his body in agony when O'Meara had pumped three rounds into his back, he had kept on running, never breaking his stride as he disappeared into the night. Who was he? Where had he come from?

O'Meara felt a presence, cold and monstrous, creep over him, followed by a sickening shudder, and when he looked up from his beer, he found himself sitting next to the very man prowling his memory.

CHAPTER 13

O'Meara nearly choked on his beer. "You…"

The suspect had sat down casually beside him, a slippery smile on his inscrutable ebony face. He was even bigger close up. Six feet four inches. Maybe more. About two hundred and fifty pounds, give or take a few. He was long-limbed but not in a wispy way. He looked like he was made of stone. And he smelled like he had climbed out of an incense burner.

Jack arrived with the detective's burger and fries and, after setting them down in front of O'Meara, shot the stranger a wary glance. "What are you drinking, Mister?"

"A shot of clairin, please," the man said in a heavy Haitian accent and produced a wad of bills. "Allow me, Detective," he said, nodding to O'Meara while handing Jack enough cash to pay for the dinner, the drinks, and a generous tip.

Jack offered a tight-lipped smile. He poured the man his alcohol, industrial-strength stuff made from cane sugar, and then disappeared into the kitchen.

"If memory serves," O'Meara said as he eyed the clear liquid in the man's shot glass, "that's a popular drink on the island."

The man's eyes came alive. He had an angular face, with a prominent nose and sharp cheekbones. "You've been to Haiti?"

"No," O'Meara said flatly. "Just arrested my share of Haitians over the years."

The devilish look on the man's face disappeared, replaced by a bored frown. He threw back his shot in silence.

"So how are you feeling?" O'Meara asked, carefully eying the man for any sign of injury.

He knew he should see something—in the way he moved or breathed. But the man sitting beside him looked healthy and fresh, not at all like someone who had just been shot up in a gunfight. He looked untouchable. Not right. And he was giving off a whole host of funky vibes.

The man ignored the question. "You must want to know who I am."

"Well, we've never formally met." O'Meara was doing his best to evince indifference, but he was burning with curiosity.

"My friends call me Papa G."

"What about your enemies?"

"The same."

"Well, Papa G, it's a pleasure to finally meet you." The detective's voice turned icy. "You know I can't let you just walk out of here."

"Oh? Are you going to shoot me again?"

Papa G motioned discretely to two men standing

near the doorway, and for a moment O'Meara thought he was looking at Max Schaeffer's ghost, in duplicate. Neither man resembled the late officer on the surface. He had been black. They were white. He had been handsome, the owner of an athletic build. They were dumpy in every regard. But each man had the same catatonic stare, the same glassy-eyed death-gaze that Max had displayed before taking his own life.

"My friends are armed for the Apocalypse. They don't care if they make it out of here alive, Detective. Can you say the same thing?"

O'Meara felt his blood boil. He was finally face-to-face with the mystery suspect, now no longer nameless, but could do nothing. Even if he managed to take out Papa G's goons, it was likely someone in the bar would get hurt or killed in the process. Considering the trouble he'd already stirred up by firing at the guy on Bourbon Street, he had no choice but to keep his gun holstered. His only hope was to force another encounter later, away from a crowd.

"I hope for your sake we never meet again," Papa G said, as if reading his mind. "But your fate rests in your hands, Detective. I have no quarrel with you. I want only to destroy Ricardo Tandino and his family. If you back off, let *me* handle the situation, all of New Orleans will benefit. Think about it. If the Tandinos disappear, so do half of the city's problems. And all the people in bed with them—the judges, the politicians, the *police officers*—they, too, will disappear. For without the fear of their boss, they will devour each other."

"And if I don't back off?"

Papa G's wild eyes narrowed. "Then I cannot

protect you, Detective. From them…" He motioned to the catatonic gunmen at the door. Were they bookkeepers? engineers? Stay-at-home dads? It was anyone's guess who they had been before joining the madman at the bar. ". . . Or any of my men."

He slid off his stool to leave.

But O'Meara stood up with him, blocking his path. "How do you do it? How do you slip them the tetrodotoxin? Do you put it in their food? Their drink? I know about the atropine, by the way. I know how you keep them alive."

Papa G offered a smile that was part patronizing and part grudging respect. "Good work, Detective. You have been doing your job. Now step aside."

O'Meara stared up at the huge man but did not move. "You wasted your time coming here, pal. So long as you keep using innocent men to wage war against the Tandinos, I'm going to keep coming after you."

The Haitian threw his head back and let loose a deep, baritone laugh. "You can try, my friend. But you will lose." He brought his face to within inches of O'Meara's, so close the detective could smell the ginger on his breath. "I have seen the future. And you're not in it."

CHAPTER 14

Billy Thune practically fell out of his chair the next morning when Detective O'Meara took a seat at the desk beside him. The big hand on the wall clock hanging above them hadn't even struck nine yet.

O'Meara, frowning at the mock look of disbelief on his colleague's face, was too groggy to think up a clever response. Instead, he pointed to the computer terminal in front of him. "Where do I look in the criminal records to find a Haitian national?"

"As in someone from Haiti who got busted while living here without citizenship or a green card or whatever?"

"Right." O'Meara had a hunch Papa G was living under the radar. But it seemed likely someone like him had been arrested at least once.

Billy stood up, stretched, and joined the detective in front of his computer, bringing with him an asphyxiating cloud of his Old Spice cologne. "As far as I know, if someone's in the system, they're in the system. Illegal immigrants don't have a special classification."

"So just go through the normal database?"

"Uh-huh."

"All right." O'Meara signed into the digital records and began a search.

"Who you looking for?"

"I met our mystery suspect last night at Jack's. His name's Papa G."

"*Papa G?*" Billy asked in a skeptical tone.

"That's what he calls himself, anyway. I'm hoping he has a record." O'Meara scowled when nothing came up under *Papa*.

"Try G."

O'Meara turned and craned his neck to make eye contact with Billy, who was hovering over his right shoulder. "Just G?"

Billy raised his eyebrows and shrugged. "That's his last name, right?"

O'Meara followed the suggestion but came up empty once again. He leaned back and thought a moment. "I'll send out a memo. See if anyone in the department knows our friend."

"Standard procedure."

It was the next logical move, but one that was unlikely to net any information. O'Meara knew the city's most notorious thugs and rats as well as anyone. If he didn't recognize the name, no one else would.

Another idea hit him. "What about the case files database?"

"It's still being archived," Billy replied. "Last I heard, they're several months away from moving everything from paper to computer. And that was *before* the budget cuts."

"Well," O'Meara offered, "we know everything in the last couple years has been going straight-to-digital. And my guess is they're working their way back from the present, because recent cases are the most likely to be relevant to current ones, so unless Papa G is decades older than he looks, if he's in the case files, we'll know it."

Billy straightened. "True enough. But I hope you don't have anything else planned this morning."

"Slow?"

"Like a glacier. Some of those case files read like novels. Doing a system-wide search sucks up a lot of memory."

O'Meara nodded resignedly. "I guess I'll have time to organize my desk then."

"Dude, there's nothing in your desk to organize."

"How do you know?"

Billy threw the detective a mischievous look. "I've checked."

"You're a nosy son of a bitch, aren't you?"

"Uh-huh."

Two hours passed, time enough for Billy to leave and return and leave again, before O'Meara finally hit pay dirt. A system-wide search yielded only one match for the phrase *Papa G*. But the name at the top of the case file left a pit in O'Meara's stomach.

———

Before Lenny Pointer had ever landed a job at Fanny's Pet Palace, before he had paid his debt to society by doing hard time behind bars, he had been a two-bit criminal and a hopeless junky, the kind of loser so ubiquitous in the Lower Nine that he had hardly warranted a second glance. At least, that had been the case until an unseasonably cool August evening in 1995, when he had decided to rob an armored truck. It was a desperate move by a desperate man, and he'd hardly made it three blocks before being run down by a certain cop in the neighborhood.

At the time, John O'Meara hadn't been much more than a rookie, a fresh-faced detective not yet hardened by a decade of disillusioning, dangerous duty. But he had been making the rounds a few blocks away when the call came. Seconds later, he had spotted Lenny, a skinny black kid loaded down with more money than he could carry, staggering down a deserted side street. A brief chase had ensued, with O'Meara tripping the suspect and watching in amusement as his loot left the launch pad and the sky suddenly rained cash.

Now, ten years later, Detective O'Meara could remember only the vague outlines of his interrogation of Lenny back at the station. In a half-hearted attempt to keep himself out of jail, Lenny had tried everything— begging, cussing, crying, hyperventilating. And then he had come clean. His confession, reproduced word for word on the computer screen in front of O'Meara, still read like the last words of a dying man. Taking the first and hardest step toward living honestly, Lenny had copped to everything—*everything*—he had ever done, from stealing candy at the local gas and sip when he was eight to selling crack to kids on the playground. He had amassed an impressive record of petty offenses, and then, for a brief eight-month stretch, kept his nose out of trouble. It was at that juncture, in the fall of 1994, that he had met his mentor, a wild man with an even wilder Haitian accent, and had been taken under his wing, groomed as a second-in-command, as a respected member of a nascent gang that would someday claim its own turf in the city's ongoing drug wars. But before he could realize his destiny, before he could go airborne, the organization came crashing back to earth. His mentor, a black-as-night Haitian immigrant who called himself Papa G, was ruthlessly murdered by the Tandino family. In response, Lenny had come unhinged. With debts coming due and his stash of smack running low, he had tried to make both problems disappear with one incredible heist.

O'Meara leaned back in his chair and stared straight at his monitor without seeing the screen. The reason Lenny had been so squirrelly of late, twitchier than ever, in fact, was because his mentor was back in town. Papa G had come back from the dead.

Chapter 15

So how had he done it? How had Papa G survived his violent encounter with the Tandinos ten years earlier? And where had he been holed up since? Had he been just as bulletproof back then as he seemed to be now? Detective O'Meara was finally making headway on a case that had begun with the simple disappearance of a fellow cop. But much remained to be deciphered. He knew the man responsible for Max Schaeffer's death and the escalating war against the Tandino clan. Now he needed an address. If the Tandinos got to Papa G before he could, much of the mysterious man's story would remain untold.

"Fanny's Pet Palace," a young woman said on the other end of the line. "How can I help you?"

"I need to speak with Lenny Pointer," O'Meara said.

"Sure. Just a second."

As soon as Lenny answered, O'Meara regretted making the call. He couldn't read Lenny's body language or study his face. The only thing available for scrutiny was Lenny's disembodied voice, which was about as emotive as a dial tone.

"Hello," he mumbled.

"Lenny, this is Detective O'Meara. We need to talk."

"Okay."

O'Meara had expected the usual indignation, a prickly dollop of resistance. But Lenny's response had been the verbal equivalent of a shrug. The detective, thrown for a loop, stumbled a moment before continuing. "Okay, so when are you off for lunch?"

"Lunch?" Lenny asked foggily.

"Yeah, you know—*lunch*. When do you break to eat?"

"Oh," Lenny replied, sounding even more confused than before. "I'm not hungry."

It was all O'Meara could do not to give Lenny an earful. "Listen, Lenny, stop clowning around. What's the name of that dive you like so much on Bourbon Street?"

"I can't remember."

"You're trying my patience, buddy. The place where you drink your fill of tea every night. What's it called?"

"Oh yeah. Chamo...chamo...chamomile. That sounds good. I'm thirsty."

"Not the tea, Lenny! The *bar*!"

"Bar?"

"What's the name of the bar where you drink your tea?"

"Oh," Lenny said from a haze. "The light's out. On the sign. Only half of it lights up."

"The name, Lenny!" O'Meara shot back. Bulbs seemed to be burning out everywhere.

"It's famous. World famous. The world...famous... Up & Up."

"The Up & Up! That's right!" O'Meara shook his head. He wanted to ask Lenny why he had been AWOL the other day at work, but didn't dare venture down that foggy road now. Either Lenny had been sick and was under the spell of some pretty strong decongestants, or the sad sack had finally fallen off the wagon, as Fanny had predicted he would do someday, at her expense. "All right. Listen, Lenny. I want you to meet me there at twelve-thirty, okay?"

"Okay."

"Twelve-thirty, Lenny. Twelve-thirty at the Up & Up. Write it down if you have to."

"Okay."

O'Meara didn't like the nebulous quality in Lenny's voice. Would he recall this conversation five minutes from now? "Lenny, I want you to hand the phone back to the girl at the cash register. She's going to help you remember our appointment."

"Girl?"

———————

"Hey, kid," O'Meara said, one hand on the steering wheel, the other on his cell phone, which was now turning his ear into cauliflower.

"Hi," his sister said meekly. This was the new Payton: soft-spoken, taciturn, and generally downtrodden.

Anyone else might have worried about her, but the detective counted it as a certainty that she would bounce back. The sun always came up in the east. And Payton always rose above adversity.

"How are you doing?" he asked cautiously.

"I'm okay. Just trying to get through another day."

"It must be recess time."

"It's still summer, dummy. I'm actually attending a continuing education workshop all week. It's break-time. If I smoked, I'd be lighting one up."

O'Meara laughed. "You know, sis, it would probably be good for you to take on a vice or two." Payton jogged every day, cooked from scratch, and pampered herself like a thoroughbred entering racing season. "It's not healthy to be so…healthy."

"It didn't do my marriage any good, that's for sure."

"Look, you could have been a saint and that jerk-off would have still found a reason to end it. Mark isn't marriage material. He's a salesman, through and through."

"I know."

"Consider the bright side. You're still young. You're smart. Beautiful. You can have your pick of a few million men in New York City."

Finally a chuckle, albeit a fainthearted one. "You're sweet."

"Damn straight. I'm also in need of a favor."

"Oh? What's that?"

"I might need to whisk somebody out of New Orleans and find him a new life, depending on how hairy things get. He has some pretty important information, at least I think he does. Information that puts him in danger. Anyway, I'm wondering if your school or the district there needs a janitor or something."

"Does he have any skills?"

"Not really. And he's a former convict. But he's trying to clean up his act. Starting fresh, you know, somewhere new, might just keep him from becoming another statistic."

"I'll look into it, John."

"Thanks."

Payton sighed audibly. "Well, I better get going. The break is over in five minutes, and I still need to run to the little girl's room."

"All right, kid. Hang in there."

"I will," she said matter-of-factly. "I always do."

A garden-variety bruiser was manning the wrought-iron gate to Ricardo Tandino's mansion when O'Meara pulled to a stop out front. He killed the engine of his unmarked Ford sedan, got out, and marched past a trio of reporters doing vigil curbside.

The dark-haired henchman, not as tall or well dressed as his predecessor but every bit as stout, raised a hand to stop the detective.

"Where's Dennis?" O'Meara asked, knowing very well that the thick-necked butler, if he was alive at all, was recuperating somewhere out of harm's way.

"Mr. Tandino doesn't—"

"He doesn't want to see me. I know." O'Meara stepped closer to the man and spoke low enough so that none of the reporters looking on would overhear him. "You tell your boss that I know who put him on his back."

The man's bushy eyebrows met above his nose as he eyed the detective skeptically. "I got a cop outside who says he knows something," he said into his headset. "You wanna see him?" He paused a moment to listen and then gave O'Meara the once-over. "Yeah, that sounds like him." Another pause. "Okay."

The man, dressed in slacks and a white dress shirt with the sleeves rolled up halfway to his elbows, opened the gate and motioned for O'Meara to enter. "Just him," he said, eying the reporters lined up behind the detective. He then turned his gaze to O'Meara. "Mr. Tandino says you know the way in."

O'Meara nodded and entered, and as he hurried up the walkway, he was conscious of the reporters' eyes boring into his back. He was going where no outsiders were allowed to tread. He had no plans to divulge the identity of his attacker, of course, and would have to be careful. Tandino, if he suspected O'Meara knew more than he did, would have him tailed. But even that was a scenario the detective might be able to use to his advantage. Information traveled in more than one direction. Which was why he had come. He wanted to feel the old man out. See what he knew. Maybe Tandino would reveal something that would lead him to Papa G. It was a risky move. Maybe even reckless. But the detective had never been one to play things safe.

Ricardo Tandino was waiting for him in the billiard room. He was dressed the same way he had been the last time he saw him—in a three-piece suit, sans jacket and tie—but with one important addition. A blue sling, a souvenir left over from the firefight with Papa G and his anesthetized army, held his right arm snuggly against his shoulder.

"I owe you a bit of gratitude, Detective," the old man said as he sniffed at a scotch with his unencumbered hand. "One of my men says you might have saved Dennis's life."

"I'm glad to hear he's alive," O'Meara said guardedly.

"You like the man?"

"*Like* might be overstating things. I certainly respect him. He can throw far." The detective thought a moment. "I guess I should thank you as well."

"Oh?" Tandino said, still savoring the plume from his scotch.

"One of your men could have easily put a bullet in my back when the shit went down."

"True. Although I think they had other concerns at the time."

"So you admit the fun here was more than a weapons malfunction?"

Tandino waved off the question. "What do you know about Papa G?"

O'Meara cocked his head in surprise. Was this a trap? Was the old man simply trying to confirm a hunch?

"You look surprised, Detective. You think I don't know who's responsible for the murder of my nephew, my oldest son, my *family*?" Tandino drained the drink in his hand without so much as a twitch on his face. No contortions. No grimace. Just an old man

119

swallowing his vitamins. "You came here hoping I'd tell you where the bastard is so you can get to him first. Well, Detective, I'm afraid we're both in the dark on that one. For now."

O'Meara laughed silently. There was a reason Tandino had run New Orleans for as long as he had. He wasn't just barbarous. He was razor sharp. And plenty charming, in a rough-hewn, bristly kind of way. Like shark skin, Ricardo Tandino was smooth as velvet, so long as you took care to rub him the right way.

Tandino sidled up to the bar and lit a cigar one-handed, striking the match against his trousers and then bringing the flame to his lips. "I'm going to give you a piece of advice, Detective O'Meara," he said as he puffed at the cigar, its embers burning brightly. "Keep doing what you do best—chasing ghosts, digging up graves, all that weird stuff—and leave Papa G to me. You got lucky the other night. Real lucky. But if you have any sense at all, you'll steer clear of this. Otherwise, if you get between him and me again, I can't guarantee your safety. Understand? One of my men might just confuse you with the enemy."

Ricardo Tandino found his youngest son lounging out back, where he was talking on his cell phone and soaking his feet in the hot tub. He had his jet-black hair slicked back and his slacks rolled up and was jabbering away, most likely to one of his floozies. The kid, at the end of the day, was hardly deserving of the family name. He was a cokehead, a womanizer, a slacker to the core. But Ricardo would always look out for his best interests. He was his flesh and blood.

When Louie looked up and saw his father, he folded his phone shut and shoved it into his pocket. "Sir?"

"I need you to do something for me. That nosy detective was here again just now. I want you and Sloan to keep an eye on him for the time being—until we can finish this."

"You afraid he's gonna mess things up?"

"I'm not afraid of anything. I just don't need any complications right now." Ricardo handed Louie a piece of paper with the detective's home address written on it. "O'Meara drives an old dark blue Chevy Bel Air when he's off duty. Otherwise, he's always in that ugly Ford sedan."

"What do you want us to do if he gets in the way?"

"Nothing. Just keep me posted on his where-abouts."

"Does he know about Papa G?"

The subject was still a sore one with Ricardo. Louie, by not finishing the job ten years ago, had cost the lives of several men dear to the organization, chief among them Ricardo's first son, Alfonso. When he thought of all that he had lost, when he let the anger rise up inside him, he could hardly look Louie in the face.

"He doesn't know shit. And I want to keep it that way."

Detective O'Meara looked at his watch. Lenny was

fifteen minutes late to the Up & Up. But O'Meara didn't feel annoyed. He felt *agitated*. It was easy to assume Lenny, hardly cognizant during their telephone conversation, had simply spaced the appointment. But the detective had a hunch that the former convict was in trouble—and that he was going to need O'Meara's help to get out of it.

The Up & Up had only been open for forty-five minutes, and the few patrons there were congregated at the bar. They were the true regulars, barflies who had nothing better to do than drink away their days in the stuffy confines of a bar where the only difference between night and day was the trifle of sunlight coming in through the dusty blinds on the front windows.

O'Meara frowned and stood up. Something told him to move. He dropped a small tip, a fistful of coins, on the table for his black coffee and then headed for the back exit. The same voice that was telling him to move was guiding him toward the alley, not the street. He had learned long ago not to question that voice. It was always right, if not always easily interpreted. In any case, listening to it was easier than ignoring it. On those rare occasions when he tried to pretend it wasn't chattering away in the back of his head, it simply increased the badgering until every inch of his body was screaming at him. He had no choice but to honor the noise.

The midday sun shrunk his eyes to slits as he exited the bar into the alley, blinding him briefly, but as soon as they had adjusted to the bright light, he spotted Lenny a few feet away.

He was leaning against a dumpster and muttering to himself, but the sight of O'Meara shook him from his stupor. He straightened and then reached into his back pocket and produced a switchblade.

O'Meara backed up and eyed him warily. "Lenny, what the hell are you doing?"

"He told me to wait for you here," he mumbled. "Told me you would come."

"Who?"

Lenny waved the blade at O'Meara. "This is my job. He told me to wait here."

O'Meara didn't like the glazed look on Lenny's face. It was the same catatonic stare Max Schaeffer had delivered before offing himself, the same cloudy gaze of Papa G's lieutenants manning the door at Jack's.

"Listen, Lenny. I want you to put that thing down. Then we can—"

Lenny lunged at the detective and took a clumsy swing at him with the switchblade.

The blade missed O'Meara by at least a foot, but it was still enough to send a jolt of adrenaline through the detective's body. He instinctively reached for his gun and a second later had it trained on Lenny's chest.

"Put it down, Lenny. *Now.*"

A look of confusion spread across Lenny's face, and he rubbed irritably at his forehead with his left hand. *"Put it down, Lenny,"* he said, repeating the detective's words in a snide tone while angrily curling his lip. *"Put it down."*

He closed the blade and awkwardly stuffed it into his back pocket.

But before O'Meara could breathe a sigh of relief, he felt his stomach lurch.

Lenny was reaching for something—the handle of which was protruding from the top of his baggy jeans.

The sickening sensation migrated to the nape of O'Meara's neck, now bathed in icy sweat, and the next few seconds—or was it less than that?—stuttered by in a surreal dance.

Lenny lurched backward from the impact of the first bullet, his face a grotesque picture of pain, dumb and uninhibited. He reached again for the gun, more determined this time. Another round, another jerk backward. He reached once more, this time pulling the gun free. Two more rounds. More ugly gyrations. He raised the gun as high as his hip. Another round, delivered straight to the forehead at point blank range.

Lenny staggered backward, his eyes rolling heavenward, and then fell to his knees, still waving the gun, still driven to do what he had been instructed to do, all quivering reflexes and unchained impulses.

And then finally, mercifully, it was over.

CHAPTER 16

By the end of the day, every cop on duty in New Orleans would see a detailed sketch of Papa G. And every hospital, library, and post office in the parish would have a copy of that same sketch sitting in its fax machine. Per orders from Captain Whiting, detectives would be canvassing the neighborhoods and combing their contacts for any tip that might lead them to the man who had declared war on the Tandinos.

But none of those efforts would be of any help to Lenny Pointer.

As Detective O'Meara settled into the chair across from his boss, he stared down numbly at Lenny's blood, still splattered across his white T-shirt. He had stumbled upon the connection between Lenny and Papa G—but far too late.

"Don't beat yourself up, Detective," Captain Whiting said. "You did what you had to do."

"I know," O'Meara said grimly.

"Papa G got to Mr. Pointer before we could,"

Whiting insisted. "But now we have a name and a face. Our suspect is on borrowed time."

"Maybe," O'Meara said.

Papa G had already expired once and come back from the dead. What could time possibly mean to a freak like him? He wasn't living on borrowed time; he was *beyond* it. With tetrodotoxin and a grab bag of other exotic drugs at his disposal, he could bend people to his will, sending them on suicide missions worthy of the most fearless religious zealot. A policeman, a high school English teacher, a former convict—each had served as little more than canon fodder for the remorseless Haitian, who so far had managed to dismember the toughest crime family south of Chicago while outwitting the police at every turn.

Was sending Lenny after the detective a proverbial shot across the bow? Or had Papa G already decided to widen the war? A name and a face were good first steps. But something told O'Meara that Papa G wouldn't go down easily, if he went down at all.

"I can see the gears spinning, John. You wanna share?"

O'Meara laughed softly and stood up to pace. "You want the sanitized version or the straight shit?"

Captain Whiting gave him a knowing glance. "Give it to me straight."

"All right," O'Meara said. "I think this Papa G fellow is...*unusual*."

"How so?"

"Well, for one thing, the bastard's bulletproof."

"Maybe you missed that night."

John glared at the captain. "You know I didn't miss."

"Okay," Whiting said, waving his hand in the air as he mulled over the possibilities, "maybe he was wearing a vest or you were shooting blanks."

"No way. His clothing couldn't have hid a vest. And I checked my gun afterward. Those were real bullets I shot him with."

"What are you saying then? That this Papa G cat is some kind of superhero?"

"Not exactly. More like a ghost."

It wasn't the first time O'Meara had pitched a wild theory to his captain. Whiting and everyone else at the station knew all about the detective's sick sense.

Just the same, Captain Whiting appeared surprised by the suggestion, maybe even a little annoyed. He ran a hand over his bald head and frowned. "A ghost?"

"Why not? He's already been killed once."

"We don't know that. He was left for dead by Mr. Tandino's goons. But obviously they didn't finish him off."

"That still doesn't explain how he took three bullets in the back without breaking his stride. And that wasn't the first time I shot him. I hit him at Tandinos, too. Hell, I probably wasn't the only one. When I shot him at the mansion, he looked pissed, like a bear that's just been stung by a hornet."

"So he feels pain, then."

"He must. But when I met him at the bar last night, he looked—I don't know—a little embalmed."

Whiting cocked his head to the side. "What do you mean?"

"I mean there's something about him that's just not right. He gives off a crazy, wicked kind of energy. Something almost alien." O'Meara, pausing a moment to put his thoughts in order, rubbed tiredly at his temples. "I remember one time getting lost in Central Park when I was a kid. I'd gone off the main path and was just bushwhacking, following little rabbit trails as far as they would take me. I went down into a little ravine, followed a dry creek bed a ways, and before I knew it, I was totally turned around. Didn't know which way was up. The sun was dropping behind the trees, and it was starting to get cold, you know, in the way only the woods can get: everything starts feeling chilly and damp, even your clothes and your hair, and you can see your own breath. I looked around me, and all I could see in every direction was trees. Sure, I was in the middle of New York City, but I might as well have been a lost hiker in the Adirondacks. Normally, when you think of nature, you think of beauty, serenity, all that. But what I saw was just brutal indifference. Pitilessness. A force or a cycle or whatever you want to call it that's been here since the beginning of time and will just roll over you whether you want it to or not. It was cold. Inhuman. Like Papa G."

When O'Meara arrived at the forensics lab later that afternoon, he found the place hopping, with Red at the center of all sorts of commotion. The toxicologist was barking orders to his assistants and nervously stuffing an unlit cigarette into his mouth.

"You gonna smoke that right here?" O'Meara asked with a smirk.

"I sure as hell might!" Red shot back, his usual deadpan demeanor replaced by jittery bluster. "Why couldn't you have sauntered in here twenty minutes ago, Detective?"

"Why twenty minutes?"

"Because that's when our star body disappeared."

O'Meara blinked in disbelief. "Excuse me?"

Red retreated to his small office, not much more than a closet, and beckoned the detective to follow. "Shut the door," he said as soon as O'Meara had entered.

"What's up, Red?" O'Meara asked warily, gently closing the door behind him. "You're making me nervous."

After yanking his blinds shut to block the afternoon glare, Red sat down behind his desk, which left O'Meara no choice but to stand by the door, only a few feet away. There was no other chair in the room—and no place to sit, save Red's desk.

"Your shooting victim from earlier today," Red said. "He's gone."

"How?"

"I don't know. I stepped out back for a smoke. The other guys were in the bathroom or staring into microscopes or whatever, and poof—when we turn around, the body's gone. As far as we can tell, whoever took it came and left through the front door."

O'Meara felt his head reel. "Red, you know the body's tied to the Schaeffer case, right?"

Red gave him a sober nod.

"So you know he was probably on tetrodotoxin

and atropine and whatever other shit Max was on, right?"

"Yeah," Red said nervously. He removed the unlit cigarette from his mouth, stuffed it back in its pack, and leaned against his desk. "Believe me, O'Meara, I know what you're thinking. And honestly, the thought has crossed my mind, too. The body had lost a lot of blood, but I'll tell you this: it was still..." Red frowned and looked away.

"Still what?"

"It was still warm. I couldn't get a pulse, but..."

"But with the tetrodotoxin, for all you know, he still had a faint one. For all you know, Lenny Pointer stumbled out of here on his own two feet."

Red shook his head irritably. "There's no way. No way! You put how many rounds in him? Five? No way."

"People survive multiple gunshot wounds all the time," O'Meara said. "Even without the aid of drugs."

"Not this gentleman. He was dead. He had to be."

O'Meara scowled. "Had you started...you know... working on him yet?"

"I hadn't started cutting into him yet, if that's what you mean. I always begin with the noninvasive procedures first. Standard protocol."

O'Meara's head was swimming. "I feel like I'm stuck in a weird dream," he grumbled. It was time to grab control of the situation. "Okay, let's think this through. If Lenny's alive and somehow crawled out of here, he couldn't have gotten far. He's drugged out of his mind, full of bullets, and leaking what little blood he has left."

"On the other hand," Red said, "if someone stole his body, if someone's *playing* with us, he could be on the other side of town by now."

O'Meara whisked his cell phone free from his pants pocket and flipped it open. "I'll try to get as many officers down here as possible. We'll search the immediate area. And we'll add Lenny's body to the Papa G manhunt." He started to dial and then closed the phone. "What about cameras, Red?" he asked excitedly. "You got cameras, right?"

"Yeah," Red said in a deflated tone. "But they only run at night after we clock out."

"All right," O'Meara said. "That's all right. We'll get started with the search, anyway. If Lenny's alive, he's got to be close by."

———

After two hours of combing the streets and alleys around the forensics lab, Detective O'Meara called off the search. The police dogs had failed to scare up a scent trail past the parking lot, which meant Lenny had most likely exited the place on wheels, not legs.

O'Meara, halfway home, was tempted to ignore his cell phone when it rang.

"Detective O'Meara," he said, not bothering to hide his tired voice.

"Hey. This is Jason."

The detective breathed a sigh of relief at the sound of Jason's youthful voice. He didn't have the energy to talk to his captain or Billy Thune or whoever else might be calling from the station. Jason, though, was another matter. "Hey, kid. What's up?"

"Not much. You doing anything?"

"Just driving."

"You wanna shoot some hoops?"

O'Meara's first instinct was to say no. He was too tired. Too distracted. Too damn overwrought. But hoops sounded like the perfect answer to all three problems. "Sure. I'll be at the park in a few minutes. I just need to stop home and get a change of clothes."

"Cool," Jason said. "I'll beat you there."

The kid was true to his word. He was practicing from the free-throw line when O'Meara pulled up fifteen minutes later. The two traded small talk for a minute or two and then went to work.

"You married?" Jason asked after sinking a baseline jumper from eighteen feet out.

O'Meara wasn't sure which to pick up first: his jaw or his jockstrap. The kid made it look easy. "No," he finally said.

"Divorced?"

"No," O'Meara said, taking the ball at the top of the key and proceeding to dribble it off his foot.

"Got a girlfriend?"

"No."

"You gay?"

O'Meara laughed. "No. But as slow as my love life is, I might as well be a monk." He tried to herd Jason away from the baseline, where he'd just hit his last shot, and inadvertently gave him a free lane to the hoop for an easy lay-up. "What about you? You got a girlfriend at school?"

Jason scrunched his face into a frown. "No way, man. I don't got time for that shit."

"So I'm married to my job and you're focused on school and basketball," O'Meara mused. "At least we have our priorities straight."

Jason swatted away the detective's jump-shot and threw him an angry glare. "If I'd known you were gonna phone it in, I wouldn't have called, man."

O'Meara, who was still chasing down the loose ball, stopped where he was and let the ball roll to a standstill several yards away. "Who says I'm phoning it in?"

Jason shrugged. "You're embarrassing yourself, man."

This kid was something else.

"I thought the idea was to just play a friendly game of basketball," the detective offered.

"Yeah, but show some self-respect."

O'Meara began a slow walk—sullen and full of swagger—to retrieve the ball.

But Jason raced past him and returned the ball to the top of the key, where it was clear he intended to hold it hostage. "Out with it," he said. "Whatever's bugging you, let's have it. Then we can play."

"Maybe I don't want to talk about it," O'Meara said flatly.

Jason folded his arms across the ball. "Maybe I won't play till you do."

O'Meara laughed defensively. "Look, kid, you called and asked if I wanted to shoot some hoops. I said I was game. So let's play."

Jason, still commanding the top of the key, refused to budge. "Not until you say what's bugging you."

What did the kid want to know about? Should O'Meara tell him about Lenny? About how the former convict, after working hard to turn his life around, had been dragged under by a drug-dispensing, bulletproof madman? Maybe he should tell him what it was like to shoot Lenny five times at close range, so close he could feel the man's blood mist his face and hands like aerosol from a can. Maybe he wanted to know about Lenny's disappearance from the lab. One minute his body had been lying prone on a table, ready for dissection and study. The next it was gone.

"Kid," O'Meara said impatiently, "unless you know somebody who can tell me about people coming back from the dead, there's nothing you can do to help."

Jason chewed on the thought a moment, his eyes downcast. Finally he looked up at the detective. "You mean zombies and shit?"

O'Meara felt his face flush red. "When you put it like that…"

Jason dribbled the ball a few times and then stopped, clearly still thinking things over. "I don't know much about voodoo or whatever. But my grandma might know someone. She knows all sorts of whack people in the city."

"*Whack* people?"

"Fortune tellers, witches," Jason said with a shrug. "Freaks. I'll talk to her tonight. See if she's game for talking with you."

"Okay," O'Meara said hesitantly. What was he getting himself into?

"Cool," Jason said and spun the basketball on his finger, openly taunting the detective. "Now maybe we can play already."

CHAPTER 17

Ginger Elizabeth Edmonds, as far as Detective O'Meara could tell, was as antique as most of her furnishings—and just as eclectic. Her old shotgun shack in the Lower Nine was deep, narrow, and, with the shades drawn in every room, a dim haven for dusty relics of days gone by. From the old German cuckoo clock on the living room wall to the clutter of framed photos and funky knickknacks populating every table, shelf, and mantle, the house paid homage to decades and people long past.

And then there was Grandma Edmonds herself, the elder matriarch of the Edmonds family. Mrs. Edmonds, approaching eighty, appeared to be one tough old bird. She wore reading glasses, dentures, and a lopsided black wig, but the trappings of her age couldn't hide the wicked gleam in her eyes. She had been places. Done things. Known people. She was a well-traveled, well-wrinkled soul—with the age spots and stooped posture to prove it. According to Jason, the only traveling she did nowadays was to Charity

Hospital for dialysis. But she still had the look of a woman of authority, someone with friends in high—and low—places.

"My grandson says you need my help, Detective," she said after setting a cup of peppermint tea in front of O'Meara, the saucer and cup shaking in her hands as she gently placed them in between a cluster of porcelain figurines and a stack of photo albums on the coffee table.

After shooting hoops last night, Jason had asked his grandmother about the possibility of speaking with the detective. And now, less than twenty-four hours later, O'Meara was seated across from her in her living room.

"That's correct," O'Meara said guardedly. "We've run into some unusual things."

"Such as?"

"Well, let's see." O'Meara beat out a rhythm, a haphazard little drum fill, on his knees. "Bulletproof suspects. People coming back from the dead. Things like that."

"Uh-huh," she said without batting an eyelash. "You want a sugar cube in your tea?"

"Straight's fine," O'Meara said self-consciously.

Did she think he was crazy—or boring? He couldn't tell.

"I like sugar in mine. I'll be right back."

"Let me get it for you," O'Meara said, taking his feet.

"Oh, don't trouble yourself, Detective. Sit down. I don't get too many visitors anymore. My daughter and grandson—everybody's always fussing over me. But I can take care of myself."

"I don't doubt that," O'Meara said as he watched her slowly but determinedly make her way back to the kitchen for the sugar cubes.

She relied heavily on a wooden cane to negotiate the mustard shag carpet, although the detective didn't have to stretch his imagination to picture her using it like an oversized nightstick on an intruder or a misbehaving dog.

She returned a moment later with the sugar cubes, which were practically spilling over the sides of a small crystal bowl.

"My doctor says sugar's bad for me," she said with a twinkle in her eye. "But what does she know?"

O'Meara laughed sadly. The last thing a diabetic patient needed, particularly an elderly one with failing kidneys, was sugar in her tea. But he wasn't about to try to stop her. She might whack him with her cane.

"So..." She settled into an old Victorian wingback chair, leaning her cane against an end table next to her. "What's all this about bulletproof people coming back from the dead?"

"Well, it's a little complicated. And a lot of it I can't discuss. But—"

"Oh, don't vex yourself, Detective." She blew on her tea carefully, but didn't sip it. "I watch the news. I *talk* to people. I know all about what's happening out there."

"All right," O'Meara said with a chuckle. "Then maybe you know someone who has some experience with this kind of thing, someone who can help me get a handle on what I'm up against."

"I know all kinds of people who know all kinds of things," Grandma Edmonds said cryptically.

"You know this city well, don't you?"

"I was born and raised here, Detective. I've seen it rise and fall a dozen times. Seen every kind of huckster and con artist try to filch a piece of the pie. I've ridden out hurricanes and floods and every kind of calamity under the sun. I've even been thrown in jail, sonny."

O'Meara threw her a surprised look.

"That was before you was born. Back when we black folk had some serious marching to do. Lawd, yes, Detective, I know this town better than I know my own soul." She sighed contentedly. "I'll be moving on soon, and when I die, I plan to be right here—in my home, in my neighborhood, with my family around me." She waved at the air, as if tired of discussing her own demise. "Like I was saying, I know all kinds of people in this town. People who know all kinds of wild and woolly things. But there's only one who can help you."

"Oh?" O'Meara said from the edge of his seat.

"Yes, sir, Detective. There's only one person who can help you."

"Who might that be?"

"Her name is Esmeralda. Esmeralda Gibbons. She come from Haiti. A white witch."

"A white witch," O'Meara mused. He'd heard the term before, although he wasn't sure precisely what it meant. He stood up eagerly. "Does she have an address?"

"She sure does. She runs a tourist shop in the French Quarter. Ain't much more than a hole in the wall." Grandma Edmonds scribbled out an address on a piece of paper. "Happy hunting, Detective."

He thanked her for the address and the tea and was halfway out the front door when the old lady offered one last kernel of wisdom.

"Please keep in mind, Detective, that Esmeralda is a bit *different.*"

———————————

Hole in the wall was an apt description of the tiny shop bearing the French Quarter address Grandma Edmonds had given Detective O'Meara. Since moving to New Orleans, he had walked by its entrance a hundred times and never noticed it, although he had a hunch the average tourist rarely missed it. A freestanding rack of tacky trinkets and postcards, all of them celebrating the city's longstanding connection to voodoo and its murky rites and traditions, marked the entrance, and a heady bouquet of pungent incense and exotic herbs greeted the detective the moment he crossed the threshold.

Inside, the twelve-by-twelve, claustrophobia-inspiring room was lit only by votive candles and warmly glowing wall sconces. On the crowded shelves, jars of petrified who-knows-what sat side by side with religious CDs and books, medicinal herbs, and stuff-them-yourself voodoo dolls. Cajun-flavored New Age music wafted softly from a quartet of small speakers, one hanging in each corner.

Behind the cash register, meanwhile, stood a woman who could have passed for the love child of

Donna Summers and Vincent Price. She was heavily made up, dressed to the nines in a Gothic-meets-the-Bayou gown and shawl, and vibrating like a divining rod in an electrical storm. But as O'Meara stepped closer, he realized she *predated* Price and pretty much everyone, celebrity or otherwise, born in the twentieth century. Her dark skin was as leathery as an heirloom baseball glove, and her eyes, sunken pools of cataracts, looked like artifacts from the antebellum South. She was more than *different*, the word Grandma Edmonds had used to describe her. She was a car wreck no one could drive by without slowing down for a slack-jawed look.

"You're not here to buy anything," she said in a palsied voice.

"And you're not white," O'Meara replied.

The tiny old lady, dwarfed by her sheer presence, gave the detective a sideways glance but said nothing.

"I was told you were a white witch," O'Meara explained.

Her foggy eyes narrowed. "And who told you such a thing?"

"Ginger Edmonds."

Esmeralda's weathered frown disappeared. "You know Ginger Beth?"

"*Know* might be putting it a little strongly," the detective answered. "I just met her. I'm a mentor to her grandson."

"The basketball star?"

Jason was good, but as far as O'Meara knew, he

hadn't eclipsed the local talent just yet. "If you mean Jason—"

"I bet he teaches you more than you teach him," she said in a low voice. Was she channeling somebody? The woman was downright spooky.

"Very perceptive of you."

"Perception is a gift we're all given, Officer. But not everyone chooses to use it."

O'Meara felt his pulse stutter. "It's *Detective*. How do you know I'm with the police?"

Her eyes twinkled. "I can smell it on you. Your gun. Your arrogance. Your brutality. But you're not like the rest."

"I—"

"You're more in tune with the nature of things—I can see that. But you still have much to learn," Esmeralda said, cutting him off. "Just so you know, a white witch is someone who uses the power of voodoo for good. The term has nothing to do with skin color."

The detective nodded but kept his mouth shut.

"So," the white witch said, a hint of impatience creeping into her voice, "why have you come to see me? What is it that you want?"

"I need your help."

"Why should I help you?" she asked sullenly.

"It's...complicated," he answered. "I'm up against something I don't fully understand. I'm hoping you can educate me."

"I don't help the police," she stated flatly.

"Will you help Ginger Edmonds and her grandson?"

The old lady scowled at him. "What have they got to do with your problem?"

"They're innocent," O'Meara said. "They're *exactly* the type of people I'm hoping to protect."

"And what are you trying to protect them from?"

How much should he tell this woman? And how much did she already know? Was she a harmless quack? A wise old sage? By sharing what he knew, could he jeopardize the safety of others? O'Meara, after weighing the possibilities, decided on the most direct course. If she was trouble, then he had already harmed his cause by coming to see her. If, on the other hand, she knew anything, if she could help in any way, he need only say two words:

"Papa G."

Esmeralda's eyes widened briefly and then narrowed just as quickly. "Come with me," she said and, after hanging a closed sign on the glass front door and locking it, led the detective behind the counter to another door. She moved like a ghost, not so much walking as gliding across the floor.

The door, closed until now and made of solid oak that had begun to show beneath peeling turquoise paint, led to another room, windowless and roughly twice as big as the storefront. It was packed from floor to ceiling with boxes of inventory. Some of the boxes were unopened, but most, judging by the layer of dust on them, looked as though they'd been sitting in the same place for years.

Esmeralda's black face, lit only by a bare bulb overhead, was bathed in shadows. "A thin line separates the living from the dead," she said, her voice sounding eerily close in the sonically flat room. "Do you know it?"

"I see it every day on the job."

"If that's so," she replied, "you are one of only a few. Most people sleepwalk through life. They only care about what they can possess: a car, a house, a spouse, a family. They are already dead. They don't know what life is until it is leaving them. They live like zombies. Like the dead."

Esmeralda spoke with a strange accent: part Haitian, part something else. It wasn't until O'Meara noticed she had few, if any, teeth left in her mouth that he realized the source of her odd lisp.

"This Papa G you speak of is only a man. He is flesh and blood, just like you and me. But he is in league with powers far greater than his. Do you know *Gede Nimbo*?"

O'Meara shook his head no.

"Gede Nimbo is the keeper of death, the guardian of the cemetery. There are many deities in the voodoo religious tradition. We fear *and* revere them, give offerings to them, pray for their favor. Many are household names and are known in less formal terms. Like Papa Gede."

"Papa Gede?" O'Meara repeated. "As in Papa G?"

"Just as there exists only a fine line between life and death, so it is with Papa G and Papa Gede. One channels the other. But he is still a man."

"He uses drugs—tetrodotoxin, atropine—to kill his victims and then bring them back to life," the detective said.

"To you, they are merely drugs," Esmeralda said.

"At the voodoo altar, they are holy ingredients, part of a complex ritual to bring about a living death."

"But how does *he* live? How can he keep on running after I pump him full of lead? And how can he show up a few days later without so much as a scratch on his body?"

"He carries a voodoo doll."

O'Meara coughed back a laugh. "Voodoo doll?" he asked skeptically. "As in one of those tacky trinkets you sell out front? I thought those were used to harm someone else, not to protect the owner."

"What you say is pure Hollywood myth," Esmeralda said dismissively. "An actual voodoo doll enhances the abilities of the owner while simultaneously protecting him or her from mortal harm." Her face darkened. "Papa G breathes life into his doll, and it gives life back to him a hundredfold. He must keep it with him at all times for protection. In turn, he protects it, as though it were a living entity."

O'Meara's mind raced. A day earlier, while talking to the captain, he had been the one looking for supernatural explanations to explain Papa G's powers. Now *he* was the skeptical one. Papa G had to be relying on something other than some ancient superstition. But what was it? Had he developed a thin bulletproof vest or a type of body armor that could be worn close to the skin and without detection? His army of zombies could be explained scientifically. So could his seeming invincibility. Perhaps he, too, was on drugs—drugs that masked pain or somehow amplified his healing powers. In either case, the spooky old lady pontificating about rituals and charms was right about one thing: Papa G was flesh and blood, just like the people he was using to go after the Tandinos.

"You don't believe in voodoo," the white witch said.

O'Meara didn't deny the charge.

"In disbelieving, you underestimate your own power, Detective. I can feel it in you. You have strong juju. You are a white warrior. But you do not understand the forces at work within and without you. Your doubt will be your undoing."

O'Meara wondered how much money she had made pretending to be a soothsayer for credulous tourists. Did she have a crystal ball stashed somewhere nearby? Did she read palms?

"So you can see the future then?" he asked.

"There are many futures," she answered cryptically. "I see them all. If you continue to hunt Papa G, your future will be short, and you will die bloody."

O'Meara frowned. He didn't mind being told he was doomed. He'd heard similar pronouncements before. Everyone—from the criminals he busted to the captain who issued his orders—liked to tell him he would get his someday. He was too reckless. Too restless. Too relentless. What he didn't like was the direction this conversation had taken. He needed more than insight into Papa G's character, his tools of the trade, his mindset. He needed an address.

"I see a different future," he said matter-of-factly. "I see you helping me. I see the two of us nailing Papa G's ass to the wall. I see you doing your civic duty and him going to jail for murder."

Esmeralda cackled, and for a moment she looked

like she could be someone's cantankerous old grandma, not some pickled eccentric. "I like you, Detective. You have spirit. *Pluck.* But I can't help you. My days of doing battle are long past. But I know someone who can."

The bell hanging from the shop's front door jingled, and O'Meara heard someone coming in and then relocking the door.

"Esmeralda?" a young woman called through the open door to the storeroom.

"Yes, darling, we're in here."

A second later, a beautiful mulatto woman appeared in the open doorway. "Oh," she said embarrassedly. "I didn't know we had a guest. Why was the door locked?"

"Carmen," Esmeralda said, "I'd like to introduce you to my new friend. This is Detective John O'Meara."

O'Meara raised his eyebrows at the old woman, and she winked back at him.

"I still read the paper, young man. I recognized you the moment you walked through the front door. I hope you come out okay in the official review. Those things are always a sham, anyway."

O'Meara laughed silently. All that claptrap about her smelling his gun had been for show. This woman was as much entertainer as she was oracle.

"Carmen, darling, the detective needs your assistance."

O'Meara felt his stomach free-fall. Carmen was drop-dead gorgeous: from her long, straight hair to her petite-but-curvy figure. She had eminently kissable lips and deep brown eyes that could melt the polar icecaps. She was exactly the kind of woman that made men stutter and fumble all over themselves. And Esmeralda was enlisting her help.

Carmen blushed, as if reading his mind. Or maybe she, too, was embarrassed at the matchmaking going on. "Oh?" she asked. "How so?"

The mischief on Esmeralda's face vanished. "He intends to go after Papa G. I want you to be his guide."

Carmen's gorgeous brown eyes widened, but she said nothing.

O'Meara needed some clarification from the old woman. "When you say guide…"

"Carmen will instruct you in the ways of our religion. You cannot destroy a man like Papa G without first understanding him."

"Who said anything about destroying him? All I want to do is put him behind bars."

Esmeralda ignored O'Meara's protests. "Remember, you must separate the man from his doll. But doing so will be difficult. He keeps it close. It is likely wrapped in some kind of pouch and worn against his body."

O'Meara shifted his weight onto the other leg, dubious as ever. "How do you know all this?"

The old woman answered only with a toothless smile.

CHAPTER 18

A ll else had been mere prelude. An elaborate introduction. Enough to whet the appetite, but no more. As Papa G waited dockside in the pre-dawn darkness, he reviewed the many sacrifices he had made during his journey back. One moment, still fresh enough to torment him, stood out from the rest. He'd had Ricardo Tandino in his sights. His finger on the trigger. But it had been too soon. Too anticlimactic. He could have chewed up the old man's insides with one burst from his rifle, but he had chosen to wing him instead. He wanted this war to last. He wanted the *fear* to last. He wanted Ricardo to feel like a terrified fox: exhausted, lost, the world no longer recognizable. He wanted the heretofore untouchable crime boss to hear the hounds baying, to sense them gaining at every turn, to feel their hot breath on his heels. He wanted him to know that Death was coming for him. No palms could be greased. No judges blackmailed. No cops corrupted. This was one appointment he couldn't break.

But before he watched Ricardo Tandino breathe his last, he had another score to settle—in this case with the old man's flunkies. They had taken delight in his suffering. Made sport of his death. But the end was not to be treated frivolously. He would teach them how to kill—and how to die—soberly. Death was more than the end of consciousness. More than a biological transformation. It was a threshold to be crossed, a rite to be respected, not something to be trifled with or made a mockery of. The trauma they had visited upon him would be returned and reabsorbed, taken back unto itself, and the buzzing in his head would finally stop. Indeed, the sky would clear. A fresh breeze, cool and clean, would sweep over him. He would be free again.

"He's coming."

Papa G nodded silently to Blackendy.

"You want me to gift-wrap him for you?" the sturdy Creole with dreadlocks asked.

"Leave him to me," Papa G said and stood up from his perch against the container car.

He wanted to see what Jeff Sloan saw, to see the world from his eyes, as he, a massive shadow in the early morning gloom, rose before him like some monstrous apparition. But it was enough to see the look on the man's face, to see his light brown skin turn a sickly shade of gray.

"You came alone," Papa G said as Blackendy and Guymarc circled behind Sloan. "I'm impressed."

"I thought—"

"You thought I was dead," Papa G said. "You also thought I was funny. You laughed when your friend backed his car over my broken body." He grabbed Sloan by his Afro and bent him backward. "You came this morning because you're a greedy son of a bitch. Blackendy, relieve him of his burden."

The brawny man searched Sloan, who was still arcing back at an awkward angle, his face contorted along with his body, his posture still at the mercy of Papa G's grip.

"What do we got here?" Blackendy said, removing a handgun and a bulging baggie from the inside of Sloan's hooded sweat jacket.

Papa G, after taking the goods with his free hand, let go of Sloan's Afro to examine the baggie. He handed the gun to Guymarc. "Do you use the stuff, too, or just profit from other people's misery?"

Sloan gave him a sour look. "You're no saint, either, dude."

Papa G smiled wryly. "You speak the truth." He opened the baggie, turned it over, and let its contents drift away on the breeze. "But at least I'm not a parasite like you, right? You came here this morning assuming you'd found a new client. Someone to keep you rolling in the shit you stuff up your nose. I bet you snort it faster than you can sell it. Imagine how Louie would feel if he knew you were cutting him out of half his business. Never mind Louie. Imagine how the old man would feel knowing that you and his youngest son are skimming him every way imaginable. I bet he would be upset. He probably wouldn't kill his own son. But you? What use could he possibly have for you? You're the sort of lowlife he would have tossed from a fifth-story window."

Sloan looked away nervously. Was he hoping someone would come to his rescue?

"Don't worry, little man," Papa G said. "You don't need to grow wings where I'm taking you."

Papa G motioned to Blackendy, and the man with biceps as big as most people's thighs grabbed Sloan from behind, restraining his arms behind his back while propping him perfectly upright.

"You watched me die," Papa G said, closing the gap between his face and Sloan's. "What was it like?"

Sloan's lips started to tremble. "Look, man, whatever you want—you can have it. Money. Drugs. Chicks. I can get you anything. *Anything*!"

"Thank you," Papa G said in a voice barely above a whisper. "But no. You've got nothing I need."

"But—"

Papa G covered Sloan's mouth with one hand and then plunged his other into the man's chest, just below the sternum. The convulsive rebound nearly bounced Papa G off his victim, but he held on grimly, eventually tunneling upward into the man's chest cavity until he had found the throbbing heart, hot like a furnace and ready to leap from his grip. He yanked it free, still beating, and showed it to Sloan, whose eyes had begun to roll back up into his head.

"Not yet, little man!" Papa G said, anger welling up inside him. "Not yet!" He grabbed Sloan by his Afro once again and jerked his head upright, even with his. "Don't go until you've seen this," he said and shoved the heart, a slippery fish trying to wriggle free, into Sloan's face.

Could he see it? Was he still conscious? Sloan's

eyes, glassy and epileptic, were finally looking straight ahead, but only his maker knew what world he was looking into, if he could see anything at all.

CHAPTER 19

The sun had been up long enough to heat the pavement by the time Detective O'Meara was unlocking the driver's side door of his Bel Air. As he turned the key, he felt a prickly sensation on his neck. He straightened, quickly scanning the parking lot, but saw nothing.

"Get a grip," he grumbled to himself.

Ever since yesterday's meeting with Esmeralda, he'd felt on edge. Was it the eccentric soothsayer herself that was making him apprehensive, or the fact that she had introduced him to Carmen, a woman so striking she could make a grown man stutter? The prospects of sitting down with Carmen and learning the ins and outs of voodoo were intoxicating. And terrifying. The detective had enjoyed little success on the dating front, mostly because of his dedication to his job, which often took more than it gave. Yes, he was fighting for the safety of people like Jason Edmonds and the kid's mother and grandmother, but in preserving the peace in New Orleans, O'Meara daily lost a little more of his own serenity. It was impossible to do what he did, day after day, and not walk away bruised.

But Carmen—she was obviously tapped into the city's shadowy alter ego. If she kept company with the likes of Esmeralda Gibbons, she had likely seen things the detective had seen, struggled with emotions he had tried hard to bury. Maybe she could relate to him. Then again, maybe the last thing he needed was a girlfriend who traded in the same dark secrets.

Girlfriend? O'Meara chastised himself as he pulled out of his apartment complex's parking lot. He'd barely said two words to the woman, and now he was already reserving a drawer for her in his bedroom.

He stepped on the gas, and a warm cross-breeze ventilated the musty old Bel Air. It was just before nine, but the morning was already heating up. Even with the windows down, the air felt muggy, oppressive. New Orleans was due for a stiff breeze, a cleansing rain, something to—

O'Meara glanced up at his rearview mirror and knew instantly he had grown a tail. A dark blue BMW sedan with sleek lines and tinted windows was following several car lengths behind, the driver no doubt hoping to stay close without arousing suspicion. *Just drive casually*, he was probably telling himself. But O'Meara had tailed others enough times to know what it felt like to be attached to an invisible tether. For every acceleration or turn, there was an equal response. It was likely the BMW had been with him since his apartment, which would explain the unsettling sensation he'd felt while getting into the Bel Air.

He was tempted to play with the driver a bit, to tweak him. But with everything that had gone down in the past several days, he knew he should act cautiously. The safest way to shake the BMW would be to simply drive straight to the station, which was only a few minutes away. If he was lucky, he'd catch a glimpse of the car's plates while waiting at a stoplight. Like his tail, he'd have to act casually, lest he give himself away while looking into his rearview mirror.

But when a stoplight up ahead turned red, the BMW banged a sharp right-hand turn and disappeared down an alley.

"Damn," O'Meara grumbled.

Had he given himself away? Or had the driver of the BMW suddenly gotten cold feet?

O'Meara spotted the answer up ahead, just as three perfect bullet holes appeared on the right side of his windshield, followed a millisecond later by the percussive pops of gunfire. A pudgy bald man, armed with a handgun, was leaning from the passenger's side of a forest green Subaru wagon while emptying his clip into the Bel Air.

Rather than wait for him to reload, O'Meara jumped on the gas and hurtled straight at the smaller car.

The other driver reacted just as quickly and ran the red light ahead, the Subaru's tires spinning as it rocketed through the busy intersection, miraculously surviving the maneuver without so much as a scratch.

O'Meara gave pursuit and likewise made it through the intersection without being T-boned.

Whether or not the Bel Air would survive what he had planned next was another matter altogether. The PIT maneuver could be explained in any number of ways. Precision Immobilization Technique. Pursuit Intervention Technique. Push It Tough. Whatever the acronym stood for, the tactic was only available to a police officer at low speeds—and when a fleeing suspect or suspects posed an immediate threat to the local populace. The decision to use it was invariably a split-second one. Ideally other officers, driving at a safe distance, would be in pursuit, ready to react however necessary. But real-life situations rarely accommodated the training manuals.

O'Meara, slumping low in his bench seat and using the Bel Air's engine block like a shield, closed in on the Subaru while the pudgy man in the passenger's seat continued firing at him. They exploded through two more intersections before he was finally able to pull within range.

Did the driver know what was about to hit him? Clearly the passenger didn't. Otherwise, he would have ducked back inside the car before the Bel Air's front right fender caught the Subaru's left rear fender.

O'Meara jerked his steering wheel hard right, instantly forcing the Subaru into a leftward spin. But rather than skid to a more-or-less controlled stop, the driver of the Subaru tried to overcorrect. The Subaru shimmied, its tires losing contact with the road, and then rolled a half dozen times, finally teetering to a stop, right-side-up, against a Jersey barrier in the middle of a busy intersection.

O'Meara screeched to a stop and sprinted to the Subaru, which was steaming and hissing but still running. The passenger had been cut in half, with his legs still in the car and the rest of him scattered across the pavement several yards behind them. The driver, meanwhile, was bleeding profusely from a cut in his forehead.

"Out of the car!" O'Meara barked.

The driver, a middle-aged black man with more hair on his head than his now-dead Caucasian partner had sported, threw O'Meara a dazed look and then put a gun to his forehead. "I'm...staying dead...this time."

"Son of a bitch," O'Meara muttered and turned away just as the first round rang out.

He'd seen this all before. Same mumbling stupor. Same suicidal haze. Same messy results. How many more innocent people would go to their graves for Papa G?

He was on a roll. There was no doubting that. But it was the kind of streak he wouldn't wish on his worst enemy. First, the shootout at Tandino's mansion. Then, the rumble down Bourbon Street. Next, the killing of Lenny Pointer, whose body was still unaccounted for. And now, a car chase and confrontation that had just added two more corpses to the body count.

As the bullet-riddled Bel Air limped to a stop outside the fifth precinct, Detective O'Meara readied himself for another face-to-face with Captain Whiting. It had been one thing to explain what had happened to the first officers to arrive at the gruesome scene; it would be quite another to placate the captain. If the suspects followed suit with Papa G's other minions, neither would be found to be the owner of a criminal record. Red Haugen would find the men's blood laced with the same substances that had undone Max Schaeffer and the others. And Papa G would remain on the loose, still wreaking havoc on the city, still seemingly untouchable. The guy was more than bulletproof. He was a magician with a first-rate disappearing act. Here one moment, gone the next.

When O'Meara entered the station, he found everyone gathered in the briefing room and the captain striding to the podium.

"Christ!" he hissed under his breath. He was about to be humiliated in front of his peers.

He turned to leave, but ran straight into Billy Thune, who was just entering. The normally fastidious officer looked like he'd slept all night in his uniform.

"You look awful," O'Meara whispered.

"Thanks," Billy replied, not bothering to keep his voice low. He had bags under his eyes and was giving off the faint odor of someone in need of a shower. "I feel like shit, too."

"What happened?"

"I was up all night with Staci. Took her to the hospital around three a.m., but they sent us home. False labor pains."

"Is she late?" O'Meara asked.

"No. Not yet. She's not due for a few more days.

But I tell you: she's ready to *pop*." Billy's eyes widened as he punctuated the sentence with the last word.

"All right, listen up, people," Captain Whiting said hoarsely from the podium.

"We've got a Category Three hurricane coming our way."

O'Meara breathed a sigh of relief. It appeared he wasn't the subject of the meeting now underway, after all.

In any other town, such a pronouncement would have instantly riveted the assembled men and women. But the ragtag group of officers and detectives gathering in the briefing room hardly flinched. It was hurricane season, after all. This was an annual ritual.

Whiting raised his hands to quiet the room, but to no avail.

Finally, Billy, who had just sat down, let go a labored sigh. "Everybody shut the hell up!"

O'Meara looked askance at his colleague. "You're gonna be a great father."

"I ran out of patience about five hours ago," Billy said and offered a ragged smile.

A smattering of grumbling as well as laughter gave way to silence, and Captain Whiting, after nodding to Billy for the assist, launched into his presentation.

"This could be the Big One, folks. Landfall is expected Monday. The mayor is encouraging people to evacuate ASAP."

O'Meara smiled wryly. Every year the Big One menaced New Orleans. And every year it failed to materialize. He wasn't foolish enough to believe the city's number wouldn't eventually come up. But if it was serious, if the Big One really *was* coming, the mayor would be doing more than encouraging people to evacuate. He would be making evacuation mandatory. He would be *ordering* it.

"The governor's contra-flow plan is in place," Whiting continued. "All lanes of I-10 will be used for outbound traffic. Our job will be to keep the peace and to assist with rescue. Unless you're sick or dealing with a family emergency, everyone's working Monday."

A chorus of groans greeted the announcement.

"Maybe Staci will go into labor for real," O'Meara whispered hopefully to Billy.

"God, I hope so."

"What about rain gear?" asked Officer Pendigrass, who was standing along the far wall. Bleach blond but tough as nails (hers were manicured and painted blood-red), Pendigrass had been with the force long enough to have endured her share of foul-weather emergencies.

The cops were perennially understaffed and underdressed when the stuff hit the fan. Lack of preparation was, just like hurricane season, an annual rite in New Orleans. Every year the coast was battered with storms, and every year officers were forced to brave the elements in their regular blues, soaking up the rain like so many miserable sponges.

"We'll have to make due with what we have," Captain Whiting answered glumly.

"In other words, we're on our own," someone grumbled from the front row.

The NOPD needed more than rain gear. The fifth district, like the rest, had few operable boats to speak of. If and when the Big One hit, officers would be forced to requisition whatever hunk of junk was floating by, for water, not wind, was a hurricane's chief weapon. Flooding could incapacitate a city in ways that simple power outages couldn't. New Orleans, which sat below sea level, was particularly—almost *criminally*—vulnerable. As it was, sewage and rainwater had to be pumped out of the city and up and over a series of levees, most of them decades old. If floodwaters breached the levees, there was nowhere for the water to go—and no way to get it back to Lake Pontchartrain, or the Industrial Canal, or the Mississippi River, or the Gulf. New Orleans was a bowl surrounded by water, a disaster zone waiting to happen.

O'Meara glanced at Billy, who had just nodded off, his head bobbing like a float on a fishing line. If the Big One was truly on its way, New Orleans was sunk.

CHAPTER 20

"So tell me about yourself, Detective," Carmen said. "What do you do for fun?"

She was seated across from him at their small table at Serafina's, an intimate Italian bistro, her elegant bronze face cast in the shadows thrown by a shallow votive candle. She had her hair up and was dressed in a strapless white sundress that drew his eyes to her bare shoulders and the jagged amulet hanging from her neck.

O'Meara adjusted his tie self-consciously. He usually only wore a suit to weddings or funerals, but he was glad he hadn't gone with his first choice of attire for the evening: a casual pair of cotton slacks and short-sleeved T-shirt.

"I like to shoot hoops," he said with a shrug, almost apologetically. He was painfully aware of the fact that, outside of work, he had no life to speak of. No layers. No surprises. He was a cop. End of story.

"What about family?" Carmen asked. "You don't sound like you're from around here."

Indeed, the detective had never bothered to hide his New York accent. Even after living in New Orleans for more than a decade, he still thought the locals talked weird.

"I got a sister in New York. We talk on the phone all the time. She still lives in the Bronx, near where we grew up."

"What's her name?"

"Payton."

"Ooh," Carmen cooed. "That's a nice name."

"What about you?" O'Meara asked, hoping to deflect the spotlight. "Something tells me you didn't get that exotic accent working in the French Quarter."

She laughed, her eyes smiling brightly. "My father is Colombian, but he stays in Haiti to make my mother happy."

"She's Haitian?"

Carmen nodded. "They met many years ago while he was on business." She locked eyes with the detective. "It was love at first sight."

O'Meara felt his voice falter. "What does your father do?"

"I have no idea," Carmen said, looking away. "Imports. Exports. Oil. Finance. He has his fingers in everything. He rides in limos and spends most of his time on the phone."

"You sound like you disapprove."

"I just think there are more important things in life than work."

"Like?"

"Love," she said, once again casting her spellbinding gaze his way. "Family. Good food. Good company.

Why make all that money if you can't slow down long enough to enjoy life?"

"Maybe his work makes him happy," O'Meara offered.

Carmen looked genuinely surprised by the notion. "Maybe," she said, staring thoughtfully at the glass of Chianti in her hand.

The waiter arrived with menus in hand, and the next few minutes were spent deciding what to order. Everything on the menu was enticing, from humble pizza to sophisticated seafood dishes. O'Meara finally decided on pizza margarita, the fresh basil sprinkled on it just after it had been removed from the oven, while Carmen ordered linguini in clam sauce.

They were halfway through their second bottle of Chianti when the conversation finally turned to Papa G.

"Esmeralda," O'Meara began. "She knew all about him."

"Every Haitian knows who he is," Carmen explained. "He is a dark priest, which is rare in Haiti. Only the depraved practice the dark arts. Few seek out their help. They are feared. Most people want only to avoid them."

"But obviously *some* people pay for their services."

"Yes," Carmen said in an apprehensive tone, wrapping her arms around her bare shoulders. "Those who want revenge. Those who are unscrupulous. But they do so at their own peril. A dark priest takes more than your money. He takes your dignity. Your honor."

"So what about Papa G? He's famous on the island?"

"Yes. He has learned to bring people back from the dead."

O'Meara, who was just about to take another sip of wine, kept the glass from his lips. "As in zombies?"

"It's not as farfetched as it sounds. And it's not so cut and dried. He kills them himself as part of the ritual. It's not as though he resurrects people who have been dead and in the ground for years or something. And he doesn't *really* kill them. He puts them in a deep sleep."

"How?"

Carmen inhaled deeply, as if gathering her thoughts. "It's complicated."

"Try me."

"Okay," she said, clearly groping for the best way to begin. "It starts with a ritual—like all dark arts. In Haiti, we sometimes call someone like Papa G a black magician. That's because of the way he uses ritual and theater, almost like a magician. He makes a *coup poudre*, a powder, which is a blend of all sorts of dangerous herbs and things, a concoction. He then uses what's called a *pierre tonnerre*, a thunderstone, to make the powder. The thunderstone is a piece of rock that's been buried for one year."

"What are the ingredients?" O'Meara asked, barely able to hide his impatience.

Carmen searched her memory. "A human skull," she said tentatively, "and other bones. Two blue lizards, a handful of tarantulas, all sorts of insects." She paused to take another sip of wine. "I can't remember all of it.

But the 'itching pea' is used. Other herbs and plants. Vegetable oil. Frogs. Toads. Two puffer fish—"

"Tetrodotoxin!" O'Meara interjected.

"What is that?"

"It's the neurotoxin in the puffer fish. And the toads are full of bufotenine, a hallucinogenic." He smiled grimly. "So that's how he turns people into zombies."

"No, not quite. That is only how he puts them to sleep. The powder is only half of it. The transformation isn't complete until he owns their minds."

"More ritual?" O'Meara asked skeptically. "Some kind of hocus pocus?"

"Yes and no," Carmen said, lowering her voice to just above a whisper. "Once the victim is in a trancelike state, he or she is open to manipulation. The priest buries the victim for a day, sometimes longer."

O'Meara grimaced. "But you'd suffocate."

"Sometimes, yes. Those who survive are terrified."

"They're awake the whole time," O'Meara said numbly, trying to imagine the horror of being buried alive, unable to move, unable to call for help.

"After the victim is dug up and removed from the coffin, he is beaten severely."

"Why?"

"To break his spirit. The victim, if he is still alive, is in an extremely agitated state. He must be subdued. Then he is brought before a cross and baptized and given a new name, something degrading. He's fed a paste to revive his energy and to keep him alive but also to keep him in a haze."

"Atropine. Jimson weed."

Carmen cocked her head at him. "I guess. How do you know?"

"Autopsy."

She nodded. "Well, once the victim has been revived, he is useful for only a short period of time—a week, at most. Eventually he dies from brain damage or heart failure or sheer exhaustion. No one can live in such a state for very long."

"Just long enough to do the dark priest's bidding," O'Meara said with a sigh.

He was buzzing enough now to return Carmen's gaze. She had the kind of eyes, deep brown and wistful, that a man could lose himself in…if he wasn't careful.

"So how come you know so much about this stuff?" he asked in as neutral a tone as possible. "And how did you meet Esmeralda?"

She laughed, her eyes dancing now. "I'll start with your second question. I met Esmeralda when I first moved here. I was penniless and needed a job."

"But what about your father? Couldn't he—"

"I wanted no help from him!" Carmen snapped, her smile disappearing. She paused to compose herself. "I was always under his thumb back home. If I asked for his help here, he would try to control me. Esmeralda was kind enough to offer me a job and a place to stay. I have my own apartment now, and I only work for her part time. The rest of the time I'm an office manager and bookkeeper at an insurance brokerage downtown."

O'Meara nodded, impressed. "So you learned all this stuff about voodoo working for Esmeralda?"

"Yes and no," she said. "Most people from Haiti practice some variation of the voodoo religion. I've always been interested in the deities, the afterlife— that sort of thing. I asked Esmeralda to train me as a white witch."

"You're a witch, too?" O'Meara asked in disbelief. "You don't exactly fit the mold."

Carmen shrugged, once again drawing the detective's eyes to her bare shoulders. "Maybe in fifty years, I'll look like a proper witch."

"Maybe," O'Meara agreed. "But I doubt you'll ever top Esmeralda. The lady's a bona fide sorcerer. She floats when she walks. Sparkles when she talks."

"She's one-of-a-kind," Carmen said, laughing again.

"You do that really well," the detective said, admiring the stunning beauty across from him.

She glanced to either side self consciously, showing the whites of her eyes, which were more intoxicating than the Chianti. "Do what?"

"Smile." O'Meara motioned to the waiter for the check and then returned his gaze to Carmen. "What do you say we get out of here?"

———

Enough time had passed since Detective O'Meara had enjoyed the affections of a woman that he found himself speeding back to his apartment. When the speedometer hit fifty-five, he let up on the gas pedal and pulled Carmen closer on the bench seat of the Bel Air, which had been wounded during the morning's adventure but was still chugging along gamely now in the dark.

O'Meara was by no means a monk. He had no qualms about sharing his bed with a woman when the mood struck. But he *was* a workaholic. And one picky son-of-a-bitch. He loved sex as much as the next red-blooded male, but not so much he was willing to jump into the sack with any warm body. Billy often accused him of having impossibly high standards when it came to women and relationships. He preferred to think he simply didn't waste time. True, he had enjoyed a handful of one-night stands over the years (always while lubricated with alcohol), but his general rule of thumb was as easy to follow as it was stringent: he didn't date, much less bed, anyone he couldn't envision falling in love with. Never mind the fact that such a ground rule severely limited the playing field (and had yet to lead to a lasting relationship). He refused to compromise.

Carmen, though, had everything going in her favor. She was intelligent, but in a feet-on-the-ground kind of way. Between her exotic roots and her intriguing life story, of which she'd shared precious little thus far, she radiated mystery. And, of course, she was almost criminally gorgeous. Sensuous *and* serene, provocative *and* discrete, she gave off the vibes of someone who was just as selective about men as O'Meara was about women. At the moment, her bare skin was burning a hole through his jacket.

He pulled her closer.

"It's so warm out tonight," she said, snuggling against him. "I can't believe a hurricane is on the way."

It was a sobering thought. The Category Three

storm was scheduled to make landfall in less than forty-eight hours.

"Where are you planning to ride it out?" O'Meara asked.

"Esmeralda's place in the French Quarter. She says it's been retrofitted to withstand anything. Plus it's on high ground. What about you?"

"I'll be working."

"Lucky you," she said and leaned her head against the detective's shoulder, pressing in closer.

The rest of the ten-minute ride to his apartment was spent in silence, with Carmen stroking his chest and then his abdomen, slowly working her way south with her right hand as her lips traced another path, this one from his neck to his ear.

"I think I have a crush on you, Detective," she whispered, her lips so close to his ear they sent a shiver down his spine. "I knew it the moment we met."

"The feeling's mutual," he said, wondering if they would make it the last few blocks to his apartment.

Assuming they did, he'd have her out of her tiny sundress before they crossed the threshold. If not, the front seat of the Bel Air was certainly roomy enough. For the moment, he just hoped he could concentrate enough to keep all four wheels on the road.

Her lips were still exploring the goose bumps behind his ear a minute later when he screeched to a stop outside his apartment. He killed the engine, hurriedly stuffed the keys into an inside pocket on his jacket, and then took his first taste of her bee-stung lips, which were indeed as kissable as they looked. As he pressed his lips against hers, he thought he heard a faint gasp of pleasure.

But the moment his hand found the wetness between her thighs, she suddenly pushed him away. "Stop!" she whispered.

"Why?" He sat back against the driver's side door, worried he'd somehow misread the signals.

The look on Carmen's gorgeous face, though, wasn't one of chastity or rejection; it was pure frustration. Clearly just as bottled up as him, she cast her eyes toward someone standing outside O'Meara's apartment, less than twenty feet from where they were parked. "What is she doing? Why is she staring at us?"

O'Meara eyed the stranger with a combination of annoyance and curiosity—until he recognized his sister.

"Payton?"

CHAPTER 21

"I'm sorry about last night," Payton said meekly.

Detective O'Meara handed his sister a bottle of ketchup for her fries. The two, along with a handful of stout-hearted locals, were seated outside at a little burger joint near his apartment, enjoying lunch. The city felt like a ghost town, with most of the population jamming I-10 in a mass exodus. The weather was muggy but electric. The hurricane, less than twenty-four hours away, was barreling closer.

"Stop apologizing," O'Meara said. "It was my fault for forgetting to turn my ringer back on."

While at the restaurant last night with Carmen, O'Meara had politely turned off his cell phone's ringer and had forgotten all about it during the hot-and-bothered drive back to his apartment, what with Carmen's lips all over his neck. In the interval between the first bottle of Chianti at the restaurant and the overheated kiss in the Bel Air, Payton had tried to call a half dozen times. Of course, a good time for her to call would have been *before* she got on the plane at

JFK, O'Meara thought. But she was distraught, and he was glad she was with him, although he wondered if she'd jumped from the frying pan into the fire. Coming to grips with her divorce from Mark was one thing; doing so while riding out a hurricane in New Orleans was something else.

"I should have called ahead of time," Payton insisted. "I just wasn't thinking straight." She offered a sheepish grin.

Even a half-hearted smile from his sister was enough to warm O'Meara's heart. Payton had his steel-blue eyes, the same sandy brown hair (although hers was long and straight, as opposed to his, which was short and untidy, always going in several directions at once). But her effortless smile set her apart. It could light up a room, melt a heart, win a friend—whatever was necessary. At the moment, it was reconnecting O'Meara to New York and his childhood. Whenever he saw that smile, he thought of home, of more innocent times, of life before their parents had died.

"Well," he said, "I'm just glad you're here. Last night was a little...*awkward*. But Carmen understood."

"She sure is beautiful," Payton said in a reverent tone.

"That she is."

Payton dipped a French fry in ketchup, pausing to marvel at the gooey results. "So what do we do during a hurricane? Watch TV?"

O'Meara laughed. "We hit the mini-mart for water and provisions, board up the windows, and then *you* sit tight while I go to work. We'll probably lose power, at least for a few hours."

"So read a book by candlelight, then?"

"Yeah, or sleep it out. That's probably what I would do. The apartment will be dark once the lights go out."

"You can sleep through a hurricane?"

"I don't know. I've always had to work when they hit." His cell phone vibrated in his pocket. He stared at the number. "Speaking of which."

"So you leave your phone on when you're out with me?"

"I learned my lesson last night," he quipped and then turned his attention to the phone. "O'Meara."

"John, this is your captain. I need you to come in today for a hurricane briefing."

"I've already been briefed."

"That was before the mayor ordered a full evacuation of the city."

O'Meara's eyes widened. "Got it. When's the meeting?"

"As soon as you get here."

The air in the briefing room was more electric than it had been a day earlier, but not because of the mayor's sudden decision to take the hurricane seriously. Staci, Billy Thune's wife, had just phoned her husband to tell him she was in labor again, this time for real.

"The next time you see me," Billy said as he stood up to leave, "I'll be a proud papa."

"Good work," O'Meara said and shook his hand, which was cool and clammy with excitement. "You got your get-out-of-hurricane-duty card, after all."

"I sure did." Billy's eyes sparkled.

"Billy," Captain Whiting croaked from the podium, "consider yourself still on duty. Which hospital are you taking Staci to?"

"We're hot-footin' it to the capital, Captain. Staci's doctor wants the baby born further inland, just in case this hurricane's for real. I can't say I disagree with the recommendation."

"Oh." The captain frowned, clearly disappointed. "Well, good luck."

O'Meara grabbed Billy by the arm and pulled him closer. "You're going to need it, buddy. I-10's a mess."

"Hey, if it comes to it, I'll commandeer a helicopter." Billy was oozing optimism. Nobody was going to bring him down. "Later, all." He nodded to O'Meara and then ducked out.

"All right, listen up, folks," Captain Whiting said, steering everyone's attention back to the podium. "If you've been watching the news, you know this hurricane's got a name: Katrina. You also know it's already trashed Florida and, after swinging back out to sea, is actually gathering more strength. It's headed straight for us."

O'Meara couldn't hide the disgust on his face. How did the mayor expect to achieve anything *now*? Ordering an evacuation at this late hour was pure political theater.

Officer Pendigrass, as usual, was the first to pipe up. "What about the elderly and the sick? Are there any plans to help them evacuate?"

"I don't know," Whiting answered. "At the moment, that's not our concern. Our job is to keep the streets safe. Looting, vandalism, armed robbery.

If Hurricane Katrina hits the city dead on, which is what they're forecasting, we'll need to be out in force on every street corner as soon as it lets up. People will be venturing out for food and supplies, for medical help, for who knows what—and they'll need to feel safe to do so."

As soon as the meeting was over and O'Meara was on his way to the parking lot, he dialed Jason Edmonds on his cell phone.

"Hello?"

"Jason, this is John O'Meara."

"Hey. What's up?"

O'Meara unlocked the Bel Air with his free hand. "Just calling to make sure you're on your way out of town."

"No, man. I'm staying put."

"What? Why?" O'Meara knew the answer before the words had left his mouth.

"Someone's got to be with my grandma. She can't travel. Besides, she's got to go in for dialysis at the clinic in a couple days. Don't worry. I've got the place boarded up. I bought enough food and water to last three days. If this hurricane's for real, we'll be ready for it."

"All right. I'm gonna check on you tomorrow as soon as it blows over."

"Cool, man. Later."

O'Meara closed his cell phone and fired up the Bel Air. There was no telling how much damage Katrina would do, if it did any at all. But one thing was certain: the bad elements in town would be looking to take advantage of the situation. There would be looting and the usual petty stuff. But the detective wasn't concerned about the small-time criminals that would descend on empty homes and unguarded stores. He was thinking about Papa G.

"You picked an interesting time to visit, sis," O'Meara said on the other end of the line.

"I know," Payton replied apologetically.

She glanced around at her brother's apartment. It was tidy enough. Just a little bleak. Other than a calendar on the refrigerator and an impressionist print hanging on the wall near the entryway, the place was a blank canvas, just waiting for someone to bring it to life.

"So is there anything you need?" he asked.

After dropping her off at his place, he had rushed to a meeting at the station. Now he was calling from a grocery store nearby, stocking up on provisions.

"Not really," she said. "Honestly, I'm a bit frazzled. Jumping on a plane was sort of an impulsive thing to do, you know?"

"Not like my little sister."

"I know. School starts next week. I should be home reviewing my lesson plans." Again with the apologetic tone. She wanted to kick herself, but she was too glum to do more than heap on another serving of self-criticism. "Just get whatever you think we'll need to get us through tomorrow."

"Easier said than done," O'Meara said. "You should see this place. It's been picked clean."

"Is there another store nearby?"

"There are plenty. But I bet they all look like this."

Payton felt another stab of guilt. Had she stayed home, her brother wouldn't have had to worry about anyone but himself. At the station tomorrow, he would be prepared for anything, outfitted with every supply needed. Now he had to look after her, too.

"I'm sure whatever you can rustle up will be fine, John," she said.

"I'll do my best, kid. I'll be home in a few minutes."

"Okay," she said. "See you shortly."

Payton set her cell phone on the kitchen counter and stepped out onto the deck. She took a deep breath of the sultry August air, inhaling through her nose, but smelled nothing that hinted at what was to come. As a lifelong New Yorker, she had lived through her share of inclement weather. Heat waves in August. Blizzards in January. But a Category Three hurricane, or however they were describing Katrina, was something she'd never experienced. Her brother seemed pretty calm and collected about the whole thing, but he was *always* calm and collected. The guy was simply impossible to ruffle. In her younger days, she had made something of a hobby out of trying to provoke him, whether that meant staging elaborate April fool pranks or telling tall tales. But he had always maintained an even keel, no matter how crazy the stunt.

John had always been an inscrutable one. Loyal. Generous. But unknowable. Since their parents' death, something in him had shut down. He had gone into crisis mode, assuming the role of protective big brother, and had been there ever since. She hadn't been shocked in the least the day he became a policeman. She had known all along that he was destined to serve. He was a caretaker by nature. His choice of location, though, had surprised her. She had always assumed he would stay in New York, if for no other reason than to look after her. But he had fallen in love with the Big Easy during a week-long vacation and, fresh out of the police academy, had applied for a job before returning home to pack his meager belongings.

A stiff breeze whistled through the apartment, courtesy of the front door being opened, and Payton stepped back inside to greet her brother.

"That was fast. I thought you'd be—"

Three men lumbered toward her.

"O'Meara," the one out front mumbled.

Overweight, especially around the middle, he was easily six feet tall, and his dark skin and ragged clothes were caked in red mud. The stench coming off of him, meanwhile, had Payton clutching at her mouth. It got to her before he did.

"O'Meara," he muttered again.

"You've got the wrong place!" she said, breaking free of his filthy grasp and darting past him. He was big but slow.

So were his two partners, but their collective girth was enough to block the front door.

Payton cursed herself for running straight into the apartment's small kitchen—and into a dead end. Why hadn't she turned and exited the sliding glass door? Jumping off a second-story deck would have been preferable to facing these three. Was that the stench of urine burning her nostrils? Her attackers smelled like human compost.

She reached for a cast-iron skillet and quickly put it to good use, bringing it down squarely on the head of the man closest to her, a gaunt Caucasian man with curly black hair and a prominent Adam's apple.

His reaction, like his initial advance, was sluggish but determined. He recoiled, an inarticulate moan forming on his lips, and then stumbled ever closer.

She swung the frying pan a second time, connecting with the man's chin and knocking him to his knees, but before she could reload, she felt an icy pair of hands on her right arm, followed in short order by the skeletal man's hands, which were wrapping like snakes around her ankles.

"Get off me!" she screamed.

The filthy hands on her arm crawled to her mouth, covering it, while another pair groped clumsily at her waist. And slowly she felt herself being tugged to the floor, where she was swallowed by a suffocating swarm of decaying bodies.

CHAPTER 22

As Detective O'Meara walked the short flight of stairs up to his apartment, his stomach felt like it was going in the opposite direction. Something wasn't right.

"Payton?" he called, hurrying to the front door, which was wide open.

He nearly ran into Edna, his downstairs neighbor, who was standing in the entrance to his kitchen, her mouth wrapped tightly in a frown and her eyes bulging with fear.

"I tried to stop them," she said in a trembling voice. "But there were too many."

O'Meara guided her to the dining nook and gently lowered her to a chair. "What happened?"

"They took your sister."

The detective glanced from Edna's white bun, which was sporting several loose strands of hair and looked ready to come undone, to the kitchen floor, which was strewn with muddy footprints. A cast-iron frying pan sat face down in the corner.

"Who?"

Edna shook her head worriedly. "I don't know. There were three of them. A man was waiting for them in the parking lot. They took her away!"

"Did you get a good look at the car?"

The old spinster seemed lost in her thoughts, too traumatized to break out of the fog.

"Edna?"

"I don't remember the car," she said. "I don't even know if it was a car or a truck or what." She offered a hopeful smile as she handed him a little Post-it note she had stolen from the counter next to the phone. "I was too busy memorizing the license plate number."

Their mouths moved, but she couldn't make out what they were saying. It was all she could do just to keep her head up and her eyes open.

Where am I?

Shadows streaked by.

A dark, wiry man. Undersized. Menacing. His aura, unredeemable and remorseless, was palpable.

Another one. Muscles from head to toe. He was an empty vessel. Harmless without instruction.

Both men orbited around the third man. Tall and rangy, with a sweeping wingspan, he was the one who made everything happen. He was dressed in khaki cotton slacks, a black T-shirt, and black leather topsiders, his face like a shadow, impervious to scrutiny. He was speaking to her, but the words couldn't penetrate the drug-induced haze.

Yes! She had been drugged. She remembered the struggle on her brother's kitchen floor, her foul-smelling attackers, the incoherent thrashing. She had blacked out but had come to in the back of someone's SUV—just in time to feel the exquisite, white-hot pain of a needle being thrust into her arm.

Get off me!

Words sprung up, like air bubbles barreling toward the surface of a deep body of water, but the synapses were all broken, the connections lost.

The hulking one spoke like a priest, delivering each word in a monotonous lilt. Did he really believe he was channeling something spiritual, something important? She wished she had the strength, the clarity of mind, to cut him down to size. But she could only stare dumbly as he tossed wriggling things, one at a time, into a small stone bowl. Was that a toad? A fish? She was hallucinating. She had to be. There was no other way to explain the dozens of tarantulas. Tarantulas by the handful. All legs and bloated abdomens as they were crushed into a paste, along with the toads and the fish and the lizards and the herbs and plants.

Oh God.

She wanted to wake up, to make it go away, but she couldn't take her eyes off her tormentor, his elongated frame lit only by flickering candlelight. She watched with fascination as he tore off his shirt after accidentally splattering it with the exploding entrails of one of his many-legged victims. He was at once sinewy and brawny, elegant and brutish, his rough-hewn chest and arms rippling with an almost electric musculature. As he tossed his shirt to the black-and-white-tiled floor, she spied a tan leather pouch strapped like a shoulder holster against his body. What did he hide in there? A knife? A small pistol? She looked to his henchmen and saw that their eyes, too, were drawn to it.

What is it? What's in there?

Detective O'Meara clicked off his cell phone in disgust. Of course the SUV had been reported stolen three days ago! Had it actually belonged to one of Payton's abductors, he would be able to trace it back to Papa G. But from day one, this case had turned up nothing but dead ends. Why would it be any different now that his sister was involved?

O'Meara slammed his fist against the steering wheel as he sped toward the French Quarter. "Goddamn it, Papa G! Where are you?"

The only person who might know was about to receive an unannounced visit.

The detective's cell phone chirped, and he hurriedly answered it. "O'Meara!" he said excitedly.

"Hey. It's Carmen."

His shoulders fell. "Oh. Hey."

"You don't sound very excited to hear from me."

"He took my sister."

"What? Who?"

"Papa G. The bastard kidnapped my sister."

"Oh my God," she whispered. "I'm so sorry, John. What are you going to do?"

He delivered his answer through gritted teeth. "Whatever it takes."

"John, I hope you're not thinking of going after him. You don't know what you're getting into. At least bring some backup. Don't do it alone."

"There's no time. And even if there was, it wouldn't matter. They've got their hands full back at the station. There's a hurricane coming, remember?"

Carmen's voice dropped to a lower register. "Listen to me, John. If he has your sister, he's not going to hurt her. He's going to use her as a bargaining chip, right? You need to slow down and think things through." Her voice tailed off momentarily. "Wait a second. *How* are you going to find him? Do you even know where he is?"

The Bel Air limped to a stop a few feet from Esmeralda's shop. For once, street-side parking in the most frequented neighborhood of New Orleans was a snap. "No, but I figure your boss does."

"My boss? Esmeralda? Wait, John. I don't think that's—"

O'Meara clicked off his cell phone and trotted toward the tacky tourist trap. The freestanding rack stuffed with postcards and worthless trinkets was conspicuously absent. In its place, a closed sign hung in the window.

He tried the door and found it locked. "Esmeralda!" he hollered, pounding on the glass. "Damn it!"

A quick survey of the other storefronts told him the old witch wasn't the only one to have closed up shop in anticipation of the brewing storm barreling up the Gulf. The stretch was eerily quiet, with most of the stores boarded up and all but a few watering holes abandoned. Maybe the Big One really was on its way.

O'Meara jogged to the corner, cut right down the cross street, and took another sharp right, the soles of his shoes stealing the heat from the pavement as he hurried down the alley.

He banged on the back door to Esmeralda's shop, hoping against hope. "Come on, lady. Answer!"

"He said you'd come."

O'Meara whirled around to see Lenny Pointer, or a partially decomposed version thereof, staring back at him.

"What the—?"

He was still wearing the same torn T-shirt and jeans from the day of their last encounter, but his head and chest had been bandaged. His skin, gray-green like Lake Pontchartrain on a rainy day, looked gangrenous—and matched the color of the tire iron he was gripping loosely with his right hand.

"You can't even lift that thing, buddy. Come on. We need to get you to a hospital."

"He said you'd come," Lenny mumbled again and stutter-stepped toward the detective.

"Who?" O'Meara said, backing up carefully. "Papa G?"

"He tells me what to do," Lenny answered and reached into his pocket, clumsily tugging free a small handgun. It was smaller than the one he had tried to put to use during their last encounter, but just as lethal.

"Here we go again," O'Meara muttered.

Had Lenny caught him a few hours earlier, the detective would have hurriedly considered his options. Lenny was drugged out of his skull and gravely wounded. How much would it take to incapacitate him? Could he afford to lose any more blood?

But there was no time to debate. He had killed Lenny once before. He would have to do it again.

In fact, Lenny fell to his knees after just the third shot. And O'Meara, leaving nothing to chance, relieved the twice-dead man of his weapon.

He was searching Lenny's body for something— *anything*—when the back door to Esmeralda's shop opened, and the old mystic appeared in the doorway. The tortured look on her leathery face told O'Meara everything he needed to know.

"You put this man back together," he said and stood up. "Gave him just enough juice to go one last round."

"I didn't have a choice," she said.

"You always have a choice," O'Meara said.

She glanced away dejectedly. "I thought there was a chance I could save him, that *you* could save him."

"While Papa G buries my sister alive?"

Esmeralda's ebony eyes registered genuine alarm. "I had no idea."

"Of course not. You're too busy playing God."

"I already told you," Esmeralda said tersely. "This was not my idea. Papa G brought him to me. I was told to dress the man's wounds and revive him—or die. I don't fear death, Detective. But I'm not ready to pass on just yet, understand? Not when so much still hangs in the balance."

"That's right." O'Meara removed a pair of handcuffs from his back pocket and, after dragging Lenny's body to a nearby dumpster, cuffed him to one of the steel posts girding its base. "I want you to call the police and tell them Lenny Pointer's body—the same one that walked out of the pathology lab—is waiting for pickup in your alley. But before you do that, I want you to give me an address."

"You're not ready yet, Detective," Esmeralda said dismissively. "You still have much to—"

O'Meara didn't bother being gentle as he pressed the barrel of his gun against the old woman's wrinkled forehead. "You ain't Yoda, lady—and I'm not Luke fucking Skywalker. You're going to tell me where Papa G's holing up, and I'm going to go get my sister. Got it?"

She could breathe, although she wasn't quite sure how—it just happened. Slowly. Evenly. *Shallowly.* She could hear in her ears her heart beating out an unhurried rhythm, as well. And she could taste something metallic in her mouth. Was it fear? Desperation?

But she couldn't move.

She was powerless to do anything as the lid to her wood coffin was lowered on top of her, the starlit night sky replaced with suffocating blackness. Each nail, as it was pounded into place, told her that where she was going was permanent. There was no way out. No mercy. Just this.

She tried to get used to the idea. How long could she live in this box? Would she know the difference between one hour and the next? Between breathing and suffocating? Would she be able to fall asleep? Or had she already drifted off?

There was something surreal about being lowered into the earth. Not quite falling. Not quite landing. It was a strange kind of hovering. As the first shovelful of dirt rained down on the lid, she imagined she was back home, snuggled beneath the comforter, listening to rain dance on the window pane. She thought back to her decision to jump on the next available flight to New Orleans. What had drawn her here? It wasn't just the comfort of her brother's presence that she sought. He was solid as any rock, as dependable as the tides. But she had needed to escape. Mark's affair had poked a hole in the fairy tale that had been their marriage, deflating not only her idealized relationship but her self-image in the process. She had always been an achiever. A *doer*. But who was she really? What kind of a person married someone she knew was wrong for her? What kind of a person thought she could save a man from his own wanderlust? Who was more foolish? The cheater? Or the woman who had tried to tame him?

Anybody could be buried, she thought. The hard part was digging your way out.

Chapter 23

It was well past midnight by the time O'Meara pulled off the highway and onto a gravel road heading upland into a dense pine grove. With the governor's contra-flow plan in effect, I-10 had nevertheless been a bumper-to-bumper mess, a white-knuckle affair that had given the detective nothing but fits from beginning to end. Once off the interstate, he had found the roads less congested but also less familiar. Now, out here in no-man's land, he was sufficiently turned around to not know whether he was driving toward the coast or farther inland. He was less than forty-five miles from downtown New Orleans, according to his speedometer, but judging by the ink-black pine forest framing the narrow road ahead, he might as well have been four hundred and fifty. He was nowhere. His headlights told him as much.

His anger, smoldering at a steady rate since Payton's abduction, only burned hotter when he thought of the possibility that Esmeralda had given him a bogus address, sending him on a wild goose chase while his sister suffered a fate very much like death.

"Come on!" O'Meara groused, wondering how many more miles this supposedly dead-end road could possibly go. Two? Twenty?

He had his answer less than a mile later when he spotted a gate up ahead.

He slowed to a stop, giving himself plenty of room, and debated what to do. If this was indeed Papa G's compound, he had cameras or motion sensors on that gate, which meant the only way in was on foot. O'Meara backed the Bel Air into a small clearing he had seen several yards back, locked it up tight, and then jogged back the way he had come. When he was within fifty yards of the gate, he disappeared into the pines and threaded his way through to the other side. A closer look at the gate, stolen from behind a stout trunk, confirmed his suspicions. This was no ordinary privacy gate. Infrared cameras mounted on the gateposts scanned the road for intruders of any kind, including those on foot. He would have to tread lightly from here on out.

Staying parallel to the road but never venturing onto it, he hiked a quarter mile toward what looked like a glorified manufactured home. The gravel parking strip out front, together with an enormous front deck, dwarfed the actual house. Papa G had learned to push the boundaries of his and others' mortality, but his bank account clearly had limits. Perhaps witchcraft wasn't so lucrative, after all.

O'Meara's chief concern, having to shoot his way inside, appeared unjustified. The place looked abandoned. No lights. No movement. No sounds. Not even a guard dog (or two) to disturb the quiet. He was about to step out from the trees when he spied the silhouette of a man against the house. The man, barrel-chested and long-haired, judging by his shadow, had been slumped in a chair on the deck but was standing now. What was he looking at? He appeared to be staring vaguely in O'Meara's direction. But there was no way he could see O'Meara in the trees. Had he heard his approach?

O'Meara waited a moment, watching for any other signs of activity, but saw nothing.

The man, meanwhile, shuffled a few paces and then returned to his chair, leaning back and settling in once again.

Was he another one of Papa G's drugged-out zombies? Could such a man be trusted to keep watch? O'Meara thought of Lenny, who had twice managed to stake out a location and lie in wait for the detective. Then there was Max Schaeffer, who had single-handedly taken out Anthony Tandino and his goons. Likewise, Henry Evans, a mild-mannered high school teacher on the eve of retirement, had competently played the role of assassin. Those in Papa G's employ were capable of a singular focus, so long as the parameters were narrow enough and the desired outcome simple. Standing guard seemed well within the realm of possibilities.

O'Meara continued skirting the road, careful not to step on any branches or make any noise, until he was even with the house. He double-checked his gun, making sure it was loaded and the safety was off.

He then patted his back pocket and felt the familiar outlines of the extra pair of handcuffs he'd found in the Bel Air. If all went as planned, the man pulling guard duty would end up in cuffs, not in the ground.

He inched his way onto the deck, hugging the siding as he tiptoed toward the shadowy figure, which was motionless and still seated in the chair. But as he closed in on the man, he suddenly got a queasy feeling in his gut.

Son of a—

He jerked his head out of the line of fire just in time, and the crowbar that had been aimed at his head sliced wickedly through the air without making contact. Resembling an ungainly pirouette, his evasive maneuver sailed him right past the chair, close enough to see that it was occupied solely by a sleeping bag. The man using it had slipped inside the house and waited in the sliding glass doorway for O'Meara to pass.

"You must think I'm blind, cop," he said as he teed up for another swing, his head tilted back angrily beneath a mess of dreadlocks. "Or maybe you been living in the city too long."

O'Meara leapt back on his heels just as the man swiped at him again with the crowbar. This guy was too fast, too agile, and too eloquent to be another one of Papa G's zombies.

"Can your cat eyes see this?" O'Meara asked and brought his gun level with the man's face. He was just out of reach of the crowbar—but close enough that he hardly needed to aim.

His attacker froze.

"Unless you want to end up like one of Papa G's worm feeders, you'll drop that thing right now."

The man's shoulders slumped as he let the crowbar slip from his hands and hit the cedar deck with a thud.

"Now turn around...slowly."

Moving reluctantly, the man turned to face the siding.

O'Meara then leapt to the offense, slamming the man against the side of the house and jerking his arms back in one deft motion. He had learned long ago that any amount of caution in these kinds of situations just gave the perpetrator time to think up a way out of his predicament. Better to disarm and cuff him while he was still sulking. And in this case, at least, the practice paid off: the man was in cuffs before he could utter much more than a protesting groan.

"That hurts, man!"

"Better than a gunshot wound," O'Meara said and dragged him to his feet. "What's your name?"

"Fuck you," the man spat as he turned to face him.

"Nice to meet you, Mr. Yu. To tell you the truth, I really don't care what your name is—or if you survive this conversation. I only want to know one thing: where's my sister?"

The man, still glowering at O'Meara, said nothing, although his eyes spoke volumes: he wanted badly to take another swing at the detective.

O'Meara scooped up the crowbar with his left hand and, after returning his gun to his shoulder holster, gripped the menacing tool with his right. "I don't have time for this," he said matter-of-factly.

He was tempted to hobble the man with one swing. Instead, he sat him roughly in the chair and used the sleeping bag's tie-strings, which were easily torn off, to secure the man's legs and chest to his guard post. Made of redwood or cedar or some other outdoor wood, the chair wasn't particularly heavy. But if the man succeeded in toppling it, he'd be in no better position than he was sitting upright.

"Sit tight," O'Meara said and slipped inside, gun drawn once again.

Though it didn't look like much from the outside, Papa G's home was richly appointed on the inside. Top-lit aquariums stuffed with exotic fish peppered the living room, which was handsomely furnished with what looked like expensive furniture (as opposed to the customer-assembled junk that littered O'Meara's apartment). The detective thought of poor Lenny. Was he Papa G's fish supplier? Was this how the two had crossed paths a second time? It was a depressing thought, if true: Lenny's new job, his shot at redemption, had ultimately led him straight back to his corrupt mentor.

Down the hallway, a shaft of light escaped a partially opened door. O'Meara approached cautiously, his senses working overtime, and as he got closer, he thought he heard the faint sound of a woman crying.

Payton?

Maybe Carmen was right. Maybe Papa G was only using his sister as a bargaining chip—and nothing more. He hurried toward the door, his shoes noiselessly surfing the plush carpet as he ran.

CHAPTER 24

"Who the hell are you?"

A topless brunette woman, dressed only in a pair of low-slung sky-blue sweatpants, was staring askance at Detective O'Meara from the floor, where she was sitting cross-legged behind a rectangular coffee table and communing with a long white line of cocaine decorating its glass top. Her bright red lips formed a perfect disgruntled pout, but her hazel eyes, not to mention the goose bumps forming on her flawless olive skin, exposed her fear.

O'Meara glanced around the room, which had obviously been converted at some point from a bedroom to a home theater. The windows were covered with acoustic tiles, and every piece of furniture, from the beanbag chairs to the coffee table, was aimed at a wall-mounted, wide-screen TV.

"I'm looking for someone," he said.

"Who?" the woman asked, not bothering to cover up. Beneath the sour frown and all the makeup, she was clearly quite fetching. What she was doing here was anyone's guess. Was Papa G paying her with nose candy?

O'Meara offered a hesitant answer. "My sister."

"Pretty gal with a sweet face?"

He nodded warily.

"You're too late. They finished with her earlier tonight."

"Finished with her? What do you mean?" He closed the distance between them until he was all but standing over her, easily near enough to shake the information from her if necessary.

She looked away tiredly, shaking her head in disgust. "You know," she said, staring up at him finally and revealing beautiful bloodshot eyes. "They were doing their voodoo shit."

O'Meara took the stubby straw from her hand and set it on the table beside the coke. He then helped her to her feet, gripping her arm gently but firmly. "Put something on. Come on."

"Where we going?" she asked irritably as she pulled a tiny black tank top over her ample breasts.

"You're going to show me where they buried her."

"What the hell for?"

"Just shut up and lead the way," O'Meara said and pointed to the door with his gun.

"Fine," she said and sullenly led the detective out of the room and back down the hall.

Instead of guiding him back to the sliding glass door and the front deck, she turned in the opposite direction, and after passing through a well-stocked kitchen, they exited into a sunroom of sorts, with black-and-white floor tiles and nothing but glass for walls and a ceiling. The room was littered with candles, baskets, and oversized specimen jars that would have looked at home in any medieval alchemist's lab. At the far end, cornered away from the back door, was a humble altar.

"So this is where they do it?" O'Meara said.

"Yup," the girl said and continued out the door and onto a back deck, which took up just as much real estate as the one in front, if not more. "Come on."

She led O'Meara down a gravel path, through a small ornamental garden, and past a chicken coup, the hens clucking nervously inside, until they reached a gate that appeared to mark the boundary of the cultivated portion of the compound. The decorative lamps, shaped like Japanese lanterns, that had lit their way thus far came to an abrupt stop.

"You got a flashlight?" she asked.

He nodded and produced a little penlight.

"You'll need this, too," she said and grabbed a shovel that was leaning against the split rail fence.

"You carry it," said O'Meara, who, with his gun and his penlight, already had his hands full.

She continued on, shovel in hand, into more uneven terrain, which was marked by scrub grass, wild herbs, and a smattering of ragged trees.

Finally, they reached an open stretch of tamped-down grass. As O'Meara slowly swung his penlight across the expanse, he spotted numerous mounds of dirt.

"She's out here somewhere," the girl said.

"Where?" O'Meara snapped.

"No clue. I don't hang out at their voodoo ceremonies."

O'Meara hurried to the first mound and saw that weeds had begun to sprout in the dirt. The next several looked the same.

"Son of a bitch!" he barked. "Where is it?"

He'd barely said the words when he spotted a mound several yards away, just visible above the tall grass, that looked fresh.

"Come on!" he said and sprinted toward it. "Hurry!"

The girl followed after him at a steady clip, and as soon as she had pulled even with him, he handed her the penlight, shoved his gun into his shoulder holster, and grabbed the shovel.

"Keep the light on the dirt," he said. "If you try anything, I won't hesitate to put a hole in your head."

"Whatever," she said curtly and, after inspecting the ground, took a seat beside the grave, penlight at the ready.

O'Meara threw himself into the work, attacking the mound with as much energy as he could muster. Although full of rocks, the soil was loose and easy to cut into. Moving it was another matter. It was heavy clay, as Red Haugen had asserted at Max Schaeffer's autopsy, and after a few minutes of digging, it began to make its full weight known. O'Meara compensated by moving smaller shovel loads and varying his posture and technique. A refreshing breeze would've helped, but with the hurricane only hours away from making landfall, it was still dead calm. Only the oppressive humidity hinted at what was coming their way.

"Why the rush?" the girl asked.

"She's still alive," O'Meara said between pants. By now he was standing in a shallow recess, the pile behind him having grown from the first smattering of thrown dirt to a bona fide mound.

"No shit?"

"No shit."

"You should have said something, Mister. I could have helped."

O'Meara paused digging just long enough to shoot a skeptical look at the girl, whose face, cut starkly by shadows, was just visible above the bright beam emanating from his penlight in her hand.

"I'm going to need your help in a minute," he said, resuming his work. "As soon as I—"

A painful shock wave arced from his hands, already blistering, to his elbows as his shovel made contact with something much bigger than one of the many potato-shaped rocks he'd already tossed aside.

"Did you hit something?" the girl asked excitedly.

"Uh-huh," he said and picked up the pace, his conversation with Carmen racing through his brain. If Payton was in a coffin, she could be almost out of air, assuming she was still alive.

He used the shovel like a rake one second, a push broom the next, hurriedly uncovering the top of what looked to be a pine box. Next—and not out of a sense of neatness but because he had no choice—he dug a small channel around the full girth of the lid. As soon as it was done, he was able to wedge the shovel into the crack between box and lid and pry it open. The lid had been nailed to the box only at the corners. Anything more would have been overkill, considering the dirt alone weighed enough to hold the lid in place over anyone but an Olympic weightlifter.

Earlier, when the digging had just begun, he would have been able to lift the lid without difficulty. Now, with his arms shaking involuntarily and his back threatening to seize up on him, he had no choice but to ask for help.

"Okay," he said and motioned for the girl to join him. "Give me a hand."

The girl put the penlight in her mouth and then helped hoist the lid up and away, with O'Meara giving it one last ceremonious shove that sent it toppling over the other side of his freshly made mound.

"Hand me the light," O'Meara said hurriedly.

He took it, afraid of what he might see, and hesitantly, gingerly trained it toward the head of whoever he'd just dug up.

And there, squinting up at the light with wildly dilated pupils, was his sister. She was shaking like a leaf. Bathed in sweat. And very much alive.

CHAPTER 25

"What's your name?"

The girl offered a smile that looked more like a frown. "Annette," she said softly, no longer so surly.

"Thanks, Annette," Detective O'Meara said and shook her hand. "Good luck."

"You're going to need it," the handcuffed man said from the back of the Bel Air, where O'Meara, with the help of Annette, had tied him. "Papa G will hunt you down for this."

"Don't listen to him," O'Meara said.

"No, he's right," Annette said over her shoulder as she hurried back to her banana-yellow Volkswagen bug, which they had used to ferry Payton and the guard down the long gravel drive, past the gate, and to the Bel Air. "If Papa G ever finds me, I'm dead."

O'Meara jogged after her. "Where will you go?" he asked in a low voice.

"I know a place," she said, smiling more confidently this time.

O'Meara glanced back at the Bel Air and its dreadlocked occupant in the back seat. "What's his story, anyway?"

"His name's Blackendy," Annette said. "He's actually a decent guy as far as criminals go. Not so bright. He's Papa G's muscle. Not that Papa G needs any help with that."

"Well, I hope he's a decent travel partner," O'Meara said as he started back toward the Bel Air. "And I hope he doesn't mind a little inclement weather."

The detective waved goodbye to Annette and then ducked inside the Bel Air, where Payton was leaning, eyes open but unable to speak or even move, against the passenger's side door. Annette had found a blanket to cover her with, although she was still shaking and still clearly in trouble.

It was time to see how fast the old Chevy could go.

The black sky was inching toward indigo as Detective O'Meara pulled into Charity Hospital at five a.m. with the Bel Air on fumes and Payton slipping in and out of consciousness in the front seat next to him. Hurricane Katrina was due to make landfall in little more than an hour. But as O'Meara leapt from the Chevy, he was struck by an eerie, almost oppressive hush. New Orleans was a ghost town. Even the birds and frogs had exited ahead of the mother of all storms coming their way. Oversized raindrops were splattering the dry pavement, and a light wind had begun to whistle through the treetops.

"I need help!" he called toward the ER entrance.

His words were met with silence.

"Okay," he grumbled to himself.

After making a show of checking the rounds in his handgun and turning the safety off, he trained the weapon on Blackendy with his right hand while cutting the ropes loose with his left.

"I gotta piss," Blackendy said grumpily.

"You can wait five more minutes," O'Meara said, giving him a wide berth as he exited the Bel Air.

The detective waved Papa G's bruiser around to the front of the hulking car and then had him stay put while he hurriedly extricated Payton, slinging her over his left shoulder in a fireman's carry.

"All right." O'Meara pointed his gun once again at Blackendy. "Let's move."

The tough guy did as he was told and entered through the automatic doors, with O'Meara following at a safe distance.

They were greeted by an empty lobby.

"Where the hell is everybody?" a dumbfounded Blackendy said.

"That way," O'Meara said, noting the doors to the ER.

With Blackendy leading the way, they hurried through the double doors and found Dr. Stowe just hanging up the phone at the front desk.

"Well, look at what the cat dragged in." She ordered a nearby nurse to grab a litter, on which Payton was quickly laid prone. "We were just about to batten down the hatches. What do we got, Detective?"

"Poisoning," O'Meara said. "Tetrodotoxin, bufotenine, jimson weed, and God knows what else."

"All right," Dr. Stowe said calmly as they started to wheel Payton into the nearest bay. "Kelly," she said to a young female assistant, "bring me two liters of activated charcoal."

"She's my sister," O'Meara said, hurrying after them while keeping his gun on Blackendy, who was trailing now.

Dr. Stowe looked from the detective, caked in mud, to his prisoner. "Is he your brother?"

O'Meara ignored the wisecrack, nodding instead to Payton, whose face seemed to be turning an unnatural shade of purple. "Is she gonna make it?"

"It depends. How long ago was she poisoned?"

"It's been hours," O'Meara said, nervously watching the doctor's face.

"Not good," Dr. Stowe said with a frown. "She's unconscious, so we'll have to intubate her to give her the activated charcoal, which will absorb any of the poison still in her GI tract."

"What about pumping her stomach?"

"Too late. But the charcoal will suck up whatever's left in her intestines. We'll chase it with sorbitol to push it through fast. She's not allergic to fructose, is she?"

"No."

"Good."

"Isn't there anything else you can do?"

The doctor smiled grimly. "We can hydrate her. Take whatever steps necessary to stabilize her. If her blood levels are still high, we go to plan B."

"Which is..."

"Kidney dialysis to remove the poison from the

bloodstream. But let's hope most of it's still in her intestines."

"Doctor," the young assistant said after hooking Payton up to a heart monitor, "I barely have a heartbeat here."

O'Meara searched his memory. "Atropine," he said, rubbing tiredly at his forehead. "It can be used to counter a low heart rate."

Dr. Stowe locked eyes with the detective, her graying hair looking silver in the glare of the overhead lighting. "Could be risky."

"Do it," Detective O'Meara said. "The bastard who put her in this state uses it to bring his victims back from the brink."

"I'll think about it. In the meantime, I need you, your gun, and your friend here to step out into the lobby while we do our job."

For the first time since entering the ER, O'Meara became acutely aware of his gun, safety off, which he was still pointing at Blackendy's face. "Sorry. Where can I drop him?"

"I'm afraid he's your problem, Detective. In case you haven't noticed, most of this place's patents have been evacuated— as well as its staff. All nonessential personnel left hours ago. We've got a tiny crew in ICU and surgery, plus our little crew here in the ER. That's it. If anyone from security is still here, we can't spare them." She paused, giving O'Meara and Blackendy the once-over. "My advice: go raid the cafeteria. You two look worse than most of our patients."

O'Meara let go a huge sigh, exhaling through his

mouth, and as he did, he noticed Blackendy was all but dancing in place.

"First we hit the head," the big man said.

O'Meara agreed to the request but regretted it as soon as they were standing in front of a pair of urinals in the bathroom.

"You gotta undo these cuffs," Blackendy said. "It's that or..."

It was clear he was hoping to force the detective to choose between two unappealing scenarios. O'Meara, though, wasn't about to be so easily railroaded.

"Nice try, asshole. But I'm not—"

The burly Creole whipped his head at O'Meara's, the two men's skulls colliding with a sick thud. He then swung his right leg out in an attempt to upend the detective.

Still seeing stars, O'Meara nevertheless kept his feet, and a second later had the barrel of his gun planted squarely in the middle of Blackendy's forehead, which, like his, was already sporting an angry goose egg.

"Very clever," O'Meara said heatedly. "But all you've done is make things harder on yourself. Now turn the hell around!"

Blackendy grudgingly did so, and O'Meara, after shoving him against the taller of the two urinals, boxed the big man in the ear.

"Ouch!"

The pain distracted Blackendy just long enough for O'Meara to unzip his pants and yank them—and the boxers underneath—to his ankles.

"Now do your thing."

The detective gave the big man's other ear the same treatment when it was time to zip up.

"Well, son of a gun!" Billy Thune said, looking up from a cherry Danish and a steaming cup of black coffee.

O'Meara blinked in disbelief at his colleague, the lone customer in the otherwise abandoned cafeteria. "What are you doing here?"

"Eating my first breakfast as a father—that's what I'm doing."

"Staci had the baby here?"

Billy set his coffee down, stood up, and gave O'Meara a hearty squeeze of the shoulder. "She damn well almost had it in the car, man. Her water broke before we even got on the freeway. We came straight here. She delivered two hours ago. A little girl. Stephanie. Six and a half pounds. Perfect from head to toe. "

O'Meara laughed at his friend, who was smiling ear to ear. "Amazing."

"So who's this?" Billy said, eyeballing Blackendy, whose forehead was still sporting an angry lump.

"He's with Papa G."

Billy's smile disappeared. "What's going on, O'Meara?" His gaze shifted to the red dirt caking the detective's clothes. "Why are you so filthy?"

"It's a long story."

"It always is with you," he said and pulled out a chair from the table. "Take a seat, man. Let's hear it."

O'Meara shoved Blackendy into a chair opposite his and then happily obliged Billy. As he plunked down on the plastic seat, he felt his muscles relax for the first time since Payton's abduction. She wasn't out of the woods, by any means, but he had done all he could. Her fate was in Dr. Stowe's hands now.

Detective O'Meara jerked awake.

Where am I?

Seated in the dark, he could hear rain lashing the window panes, which were groaning in unison with the rest of the building.

"What's going on?"

"Relax, John," someone said in a familiar voice. "The power went out. That's all."

O'Meara squinted to his right and saw Billy seated beside him, his face and body not much more than a silhouette, courtesy of the early morning light coming through the hospital cafeteria's long bank of windows. Blackendy was still sitting across from him, his head resting on the table, arms still cuffed behind him.

The detective rubbed at his eyes. "He asleep?"

"You both nodded off about a half hour ago," Billy said. "I thought *I* was tired."

O'Meara paused to listen to the wind raging outside. "Sounds rough out there."

"It hit a little after six. This is the real deal."

"You want to check on Staci and little Stephanie?"

"I sure do," Billy said and took his feet. "You okay watching him?"

"Yeah, but I'd like to grab a bite first."

"Okay." Billy sat back down. "But make it fast."

O'Meara stood up, stretched his aching limbs, and

slowly made his way to the counter. He grabbed a couple of apples, one for him and one for his prisoner, a few sandwiches—not bothering to read the labels on the cellophane wrap, and then liberated a couple of bottled waters from the cooler.

"Who do I pay?" he hollered, turning back toward Billy, who was still seated at the table. It was tough to hear or be heard above the howling wind.

"Throw some money in the tip jar!" Billy called back. "That's what I did!"

"All right," O'Meara said with a shrug and tossed a twenty in the tip jar.

The yelling was enough to wake Blackendy.

"You hungry?" O'Meara asked after returning to the table.

The burly Creole glared at him. "How am I supposed to eat that shit with my arms handcuffed behind my back?"

"Right," O'Meara said, twisting his lips to one side as he thought over the dilemma. The last thing he wanted was a replay of the bathroom incident.

He returned a moment later with a straw and a pint of chocolate milk. "This will have to do. Hope you're not lactose intolerant."

Blackendy glowered at him once more and then, embracing his fate, greedily sucked down the nourishment before O'Meara could unwrap one of his sandwiches. It was the first thing either man had put in his stomach since the night before.

O'Meara followed suit, making quick work of the sandwiches and then polishing off both apples.

They got up to leave, and O'Meara suggested he

and his prisoner escort Billy up to the maternity ward.

"Actually, Staci and the baby are in the ICU," Billy said. "The maternity ward was being evacuated when we got here."

As they were walking to the fire escape to take the stairs up to the ICU, two orderlies were hurrying the other way, toward the exits.

"Where are y'all headed?" Billy asked.

"Outside," one of the orderlies said nervously. "We have to get the backup generators running. We've got patients on ventilators and dialysis machines—you name it. They'll be in bad shape without power."

O'Meara eyed Billy in the dim corridor. It was obvious he was thinking the same thing. Without power, Payton, Staci, and the baby were all at risk.

"Where are the generators?" the detective asked. "We'll get them running."

Blackendy glanced wide-eyed from O'Meara to the glass front doors, which were threatening to blow off their hinges, or shatter, whichever came first. "You crazy, man? I ain't going out there."

"It's really bad," confirmed one of the orderlies, a stooped man with thick glasses and a mostly bald head. "We just got word of windows blowing out on the fourth floor."

"Just tell us where the generators are," O'Meara said firmly. "The hospital needs you two inside."

Once armed with directions, instructions, and a set of keys to the generators, O'Meara led the way outside, forcing the doors open and stepping into a thunderous wind that was roaring through the city like a runaway freight train. Trees were snapping everywhere, power lines were arcing in the gray morning light, and everything on the ground—from pine cones to discarded pop cans—was potentially lethal shrapnel.

"Let's get this shit done!" Billy hollered into the horizontal rain.

O'Meara gave him the thumbs up, and they hurried around to the back of the hospital, moving as fast as they could in a wind that repeatedly stood them upright, its sheer force enough to take the detective's breath away. He felt sapped of nearly all his strength by the time they reached the generators, which were located in a relatively sheltered corner behind the towering old building.

"This is it!" O'Meara yelled, his words yanked into oblivion by the relentless wind.

The locks were slick with rain, but he made quick work of them and, following the instructions he had been given, kicked the generators into gear, which wasn't much more complicated than turning on a car, aside from a couple of extra switches.

Back inside, all three men paused in the lobby to catch their breath.

"You didn't solve nothing," Blackendy said grimly between pants, his rain-soaked dreadlocks hanging in his eyes. "Those generators are on the ground floor, man. As soon as the floodwaters come, this place will be in the dark all over again."

"Who says it's gonna flood?" O'Meara snapped.

"My man, Papa G. He's seen it coming. Look around you. This is the beginning of the Apocalypse."

Billy rolled his eyes, but O'Meara had a hunch things could indeed get much worse.

Before anyone could respond, the double doors to the ER opened and Dr. Stowe appeared. "Detective," she called over the unbroken hum, "your sister's awake."

~~~

Payton lay still, save for her right index finger, which, while hooked up to the heart monitor, was nervously dancing to a stuttering beat, audible only to her. Most of her long, sandy brown hair, slick with sweat, was wedged between her head and her pillow.

But as bad as she looked, Detective O'Meara found himself breathing a sigh of relief.

"How do you feel?" he asked.

"Like I'm slowly waking up from a really bad dream," she said, her voice a weak rasp.

O'Meara drew the curtain closed around them and then sat down beside her. "Tell me about it."

"I keep wishing this wasn't real," she said with a shudder, "that it didn't happen. Jesus, John, they buried me in the ground! I was numb all over, and then I felt like…like my body was floating. But I couldn't move. I couldn't speak." A tear streaked down her cheek.

"You're safe now," O'Meara said just as the building groaned again in the wind.

His little sister threw him a skeptical look. "You sure about that?"

They sat quietly for a few minutes, with Payton appearing to drift in and out of sleep.

Then she reached for his hand, her eyes narrowing. "I know where he is."

Chapter 26

Outside, the Superdome appeared bludgeoned. Numerous white roof tiles had been blown off, revealing an ugly, ravaged profile. Inside, where upward of ten thousand people were camped out, it looked nothing like a sports stadium. With the power gone and Hurricane Katrina still assaulting the city, the huge building was rattling like an arc ready to float away—if it didn't sink first. A small lake had begun to form at the fifty-yard line, above which rain and daylight poured in through a massive fissure in the roof. The air was muggy and oppressive.

Of the bedraggled refugees huddled in its dim bowels, Detective O'Meara counted precious few law-and-order types. There were a handful of soldiers from the National Guard, most of whom were overseeing distribution of food and water or policing an ad hoc medical station. The bulk of their ranks, O'Meara had learned, were still holed up at the Jackson Barracks in the Ninth Ward, six miles away and wedged perfectly between the banks of the Mississippi and Lake

Pontchartrain. The detective thought of Blackendy's ominous warning—that floodwaters were sure to doom the city—and hoped something other than an onrushing wall of water would prompt the guardsmen to leave their barracks.

Perhaps taking a cue from their yet-to-be-deployed comrades, the soldiers at the Superdome were maintaining their own camp away from the riffraff and hardly interacting with the locals. It would have been better to have a large police presence, to use people who knew the citizens. But O'Meara could count on one hand the number of NOPD officers among the refugees at the Superdome. Where was everybody? He had tried to use his cell phone to call the station, to warn Captain Whiting and the others of what Papa G had planned, but he was unable to make a connection. Cell phones had gone down simultaneously with the landlines. One guardsman he had spoken with had apparently had sporadic success sending out messages on his BlackBerry, but all other communication had been stymied.

In any case, the rain-soaked Astroturf and partially filled stands encircling it provided a reasonably safe shelter from the waning hurricane outside, in contrast to the dark corridors that ringed the dome. A strong stench had already begun to emanate from the bathrooms, past which no one dared wander. For beyond them lay a blacked-out labyrinth of causeways and ramps, a claustrophobically murky zone penetrated only occasionally by the errant beam of a flashlight. This was surely where Papa G and his men would be lurking, but as O'Meara probed deeper into one of the dark recesses on the upper level, he hoped his sister had misheard her captors. Papa G, if he indeed planned to lure Tandino and his men here for a final showdown, couldn't have picked a better place to unleash his army of slow-footed-but-determined zombies.

O'Meara had briefly considered enlisting help. But he was facing an all-too familiar conundrum: although he could produce a badge to prove his credentials, his fantastic story would undermine the effort. He would most likely elicit a bemused, if somewhat annoyed, response. Who had time for a war between zombies and the mafia when there were real problems to worry about, like a shortage of fresh water and an overabundance of human waste?

O'Meara picked up the pace when he heard what sounded like the muffled cry of a woman up ahead. Papa G wasn't the only one who would be taking advantage of the chaos; other equally unscrupulous men would be prowling these corridors for would-be victims.

"Help!"

As the words rang out in the darkness, they could provoke only one response. But just as the detective sprang into action, he felt himself being lifted off the ground. Briefly disoriented, he quickly recognized the human wrecking ball—or was he a crane?—hoisting him into the air.

"Dennis!" he whispered as he traced the hand clutching his collar to the barely visible face staring back at him.

The no-neck butler smiled nonchalantly but

said nothing. As stoic as ever, he was only partially succeeding in masking the pain that had to be riddling his body. He was upright and no longer on death's door, but surely he was still suffering from the wounds he had sustained in the clash at Tandino's estate not so many days ago.

He silently motioned for O'Meara to arm himself and then, as stealthy as a big cat, disappeared into the darkness.

Was the voice up ahead a decoy? Bait? O'Meara did as the butler had instructed and readied his gun, making sure it was loaded and the safety was off. He then tucked in behind a cement column and waited.

But as the first round touched off and the shooting quickly escalated into a dizzying firefight every bit as deadly as the first battle between Tandino and Papa G, the detective found himself rooted in place. It wasn't fear that told him to stay put, but common sense. Did he really want to stop Papa G from destroying the Tandinos? Or vice versa? The latter seemed unlikely, unfortunately, considering the Haitian's seemingly bulletproof constitution.

Getting wounded or killed in the anarchy unfolding around him, on the other hand, struck O'Meara as quite possible. The cement concourse, which had been dark only moments earlier, was being lit up like a strobe-lit dance club—or a luckless fireworks stand on the Fourth of July—and through the smoke and haze and the sheets of tracers and live rounds, O'Meara could see countless individuals going down. Had Papa G sprung a trap on Tandino's men? Or was this a perfect ambush in reverse? It was impossible to tell. What *was* clear was that others, whether from the National Guard or the NOPD, would shortly be joining the fight. It was anyone's guess how many citizens down in the bleachers were armed, as well.

Was Tandino in this mess? Maybe. Papa G? Doubtful. Perhaps he had shown his face long enough to lure Tandino and his men into a trap, but now he would be trying to make a stealthy exit, which was exactly what O'Meara was preparing to do. If the detective tried to sneak deeper into the concourse, he would be heading straight into the kill zone. But if he tried to retreat the way he had come, he would likely run into whoever was rushing to join the fight.

O'Meara searched his immediate surroundings and saw that he wasn't the only one who had taken up residence behind something solid. Shadowy figures fired their weapons from behind metal garbage bins, empty kiosks—whatever was available. O'Meara's eyes came to rest on a hefty metal cart that had been left against the inside wall. Only twenty or so feet separated it from the nearest exit, whose gray-blue opening stood like a portal out of the darkness. If anyone was seated near the entrance, certainly they could see and hear the fighting going on inside the concourse. Had they cleared away from the aisle? Would he draw fire into the dome proper if he used the exit?

He bolted toward the metal cart, a plan still forming in his mind as the rounds whizzed by his ears, and as soon as he had the rubber handles in his grip, gave the cart a mighty shove toward the darkness and then sprinted in the opposite direction, toward the exit.

The idea was to draw fire away from the exit, where O'Meara was hurtling his body, and toward the cart, which should have been several yards away by now and rumbling down the concourse. Unfortunately, one of the front wheels, tucked beneath the cart and pointing askew, had jammed the contraption's forward movement, spun it sideways, and helped topple it only a few feet from where O'Meara had pushed it. Every handgun, shotgun, and automatic rifle in the concourse turned on the cart, and fire poured in from multiple directions. O'Meara, his ears deafened by the volley, dropped down low and went into a belly-first slide that carried him through the exit and shoulder-first into the handrail that split the stairs dissecting the bleachers. From there, he rolled left, away from the opening, and kept moving until he was well clear, finally coming to a stop at the feet of an elderly African-American gentleman who was reading the morning paper with a flashlight and wholly unaware that he was the only person within a hundred feet of the exit sitting upright, everyone else having cleared the area or hidden behind their seats.

"What are you doing down there, young man?" the old man asked with a hint of amusement in his voice.

O'Meara sat upright and gingerly dusted himself off. Nothing was broken, as far as he could tell. But everything hurt.

"Just getting my exercise," he answered, wincing.

"Eh?' the old man said and cupped his ear toward O'Meara, who was standing now.

Smiling sheepishly, O'Meara opened his mouth to reply when, out of the corner of his eye, he caught sight of a hulking man racing ghostlike down the stairs several rows down and two aisles across from where he stood. He would recognize that effortless gait anywhere.

"Gotta run!" he said and clambered over a pair of seats on his way back to the aisle.

The stairs, short and shallow, were impossible to negotiate quickly, especially in the faint light, and O'Meara, hoping to make up time at the bottom of the first section, deftly climbed and cleared in one fluid motion the guardrail separating him from the next section, landing several feet below on hard cement. As he ran, he kept an eye on Papa G, still a slippery phantom and threatening to disappear from sight the moment he entered the concourse beneath them. Rather than try to follow in Papa G's footsteps, O'Meara exited onto the lower concourse through the aisle closest to him and then raced toward the main entrance.

It was the only way in or out, and sure enough, Papa G emerged from an aisle up ahead and easily beat O'Meara to the long row of doors. The dark priest threw the detective a devilish grin and then disappeared outside.

Only seconds behind, O'Meara shot headlong into the wind and rain a moment later and found the going outside, though easier than before, difficult. The wind, blowing in gusts of seventy miles or more an hour, could still stand a person up when at its peak.

Alone in the vast parking lot and clearly one of few souls in the city intrepid enough to brave the elements, Papa G slowed to the pace of a long-distance runner. He was loping now, no doubt letting O'Meara keep him in his sights as he knifed through the wind.

Where the hell is he going?

The rangy Haitian strode past the last of the parked cars and veered east, down a broad avenue, and soon was chewing up one block after another. This was no replay of the rumble down Bourbon Street, for Papa G was leading the detective *away* from the crowds, down a long, almost imperceptible descent, toward the poorest neighborhood in New Orleans.

CHAPTER 27

Debris from blown-over garbage cans littered the streets, and century-old trees, cut in half by the hurricane's gale-force winds just minutes earlier, lay like contorted carcasses across roofs, fences, and car tops. But Detective O'Meara, preoccupied with his own pain, hardly noticed. With his lungs on fire and his quads burning up like the Space Shuttle on reentry, he knew the only thing to do was to relax, to give in to the agony. The only way past it was *through* it.

But the longer he ran into the wind and rain, the more foolish he felt. Every wobbly stride, every desperate breath was a reminder that he had sprinted right past his Bel Air at the beginning of this marathon. At the time, he could have hopped into his car and tracked Papa G on four wheels. But he had assumed that the lunatic was leading him somewhere nearby, that soon he would turn to face him. Instead, the man simply ran. On and on he ran, loping through the Central Business District, the French Quarter, Marigny, and Bywater, where he had lumbered right down the middle of St. Claude Avenue's four-lane drawbridge, crossing the churning Industrial Canal without slowing down. Had this been a ten-kilometer fun run, the finish line would be looming just up ahead. Instead, they were merely following Flood Street into the Lower Nine, the latest neighborhood in their mad tour of the desolate, windblown city.

O'Meara had never been much of a runner. Or an exerciser. He shot hoops. Chased down criminals. Once in a great while enjoyed an all-night romp in the sack. But he had never worked up a sweat merely for its own sake, instead viewing joggers, cyclists, and other fitness fanatics with the condescension of a man who knew he could do better—if he felt so inclined, if he had no life. But now here he was, trailing after Papa G with no hope of catching him and no choice but to continue on, lest he get away. The alternative— stopping—was unthinkable.

Is it?

As soon as the thought entered O'Meara's mind, it was impossible to turn away. Papa G was no longer orchestrating the bloodletting back at the Superdome. He could inflict little damage here, in the Ninth Ward, where no one yet stirred and nothing of value was housed. This was O'Meara's home turf, *his* beat. He knew the locals could more than hold their own. So why keep running?

He stopped abruptly, and the pain, hardly manageable before, doubled him over, leaving him bent and spent, his hands on his knees, his lungs gulping for air. Two equally pressing urges—to throw up or to collapse on the asphalt—fought for his attention, but as a sickly sensation crept down his spine, he immediately understood it had nothing to do with overexertion or poor fitness.

He straightened, still grimacing, and faced Papa G, who was now less than twenty feet away and strutting closer.

"Is that all you have, Detective?" the lanky Haitian taunted. "After all I've put you through? That's all you have?" He shook his head in disgust. "I killed your sister. Yet you give up this easily. Imagine how the world would look had I let Tandino get away with what he did to me."

"You don't know what you're talking about," O'Meara said between gasps.

"What?" Papa G said with a sneer, in his face now. "I can't hear you."

"I said," O'Meara repeated, still struggling for air, "you don't know what the hell you're talking about."

"No? Enlighten me, then."

"For starters, my sister's alive. I dug her up, right after I cuffed your guard dog."

Papa G's eyes narrowed as a disbelieving frown spread across his angular face. "The old witch!" he hissed. "I let her live!" He turned away angrily, broodingly.

But he didn't sulk long. Before O'Meara could react, he had his hands around the detective's throat and was lifting him off his feet. "It didn't have to end this way, you know. You could have let me be. You could have let me rid the city of its scum. No one else had to suffer!"

O'Meara tried to choke out a response, but he

couldn't breathe, much less talk. Papa G's hands formed the perfect vise: unyielding, unforgiving, and as hard as steel.

Just as O'Meara's vision began to blur, he felt himself scooting across the asphalt on his back, having been tossed down the middle of the street like a rag doll. Before he could retake his feet, Papa G had him again by his shirt collar and was hurling him against a chain-link fence, the top of the fencing digging into his back.

"The problem with you, Detective," Papa G said, delivering a withering right hook to the chin, "is that you lack imagination."

O'Meara felt his teeth slam down on his tongue. He wanted to roll with the blow, to evade and regroup, but the powerful Haitian held him by the front of his shirt with one hand while continuing to rain down blows with the other. O'Meara thought he heard something crack as Papa G slammed his fist into his ribs.

"You can't see the energy all around you, the connections between us. You're blind."

Another punishing blow, this one to the face, just above his right eye.

"I was going to spare you. Just like I let the witch live. But you've taught me a valuable lesson. Mercy is for the weak."

O'Meara's head whipped back involuntarily as he reeled from a vicious uppercut, and as his mouth filled with warm blood, he thought of Esmeralda, the supposedly good witch, and her ramblings about Papa G's voodoo doll. Was that what protected him? Was that the source of his strength? Did he really wear one against his body?

With his right eye already swelling shut, O'Meara could nevertheless see more of Papa G than he wanted to. The dark priest was standing over him and brandishing a switchblade, its sharp edge gleaming. O'Meara searched the Haitian's tight black T-shirt for a bulge of some kind, but saw no signs of a hidden charm.

"A few days ago, I showed a man his heart while it was still beating," Papa G said, glowering down at O'Meara. "I pulled it out with my bare hand. Yours I'm going to cut out."

He pulled O'Meara to his feet and jerked him close. "What? No fancy barbs? No witty repartee?"

O'Meara, shrinking from the overpowering ginger on Papa G's breath, glared back at him but said nothing.

"Tongue-tied?" Papa G asked and teased O'Meara with the blade, tracing the detective's jugular with it. "We'll see how brave you are with my knife in you."

Maybe O'Meara didn't know how to run. Maybe he was blind to whatever whacked-out world Papa G lived in. And maybe he was a lousy conversationalist. But he had just gotten his second wind. He celebrated by crushing Papa G's family jewels with his right knee.

With Papa G no longer in his face—he was doubled over and coughing in pain—O'Meara had time to go for his gun, which he put to good use as soon as the Haitian stood upright, emptying his clip point-blank into the huge man's chest.

"You're not immortal," O'Meara said as Papa G stumbled backward, "you're just another freak."

Papa G grimaced, his bloodshot eyes boiling over with rage, and then slowly righted himself. He looked down at the switchblade, still in his right hand, and then forced a grin as he locked eyes with the detective. "I'm going to cut you into a thousand little pieces."

O'Meara opened his mouth to respond but stopped, suddenly realizing he was standing in six inches of water. "What the—?"

An earthshaking boom, percussive like a gunshot but as deep as rolling thunder, rattled the windows of every house on the block, and manhole covers, one after another, began popping into the air, each lifted by a geyser of sewer water. Moments later, a roiling wall of water was rumbling down the street and headed straight for them.

The levees had been breached.

Papa G's eyes widened with fear, and then he disappeared, pulled under by the water. Had he not been sucked under a split second later, O'Meara might have relished the sight. Instead, he was struggling for the surface, all the while being hurled forward with the current, powerless to do anything but go along for the ride.

He surfaced just in time to duck back under, barely avoiding decapitation by a tree limb, and when he emerged a second time from the water, he spotted Papa G a few yards ahead, desperately clinging to someone's porch roof.

O'Meara propelled himself directly at Papa G and pulled him back into the churning water. It was obvious the Haitian couldn't swim, and O'Meara was going to make him pay.

"Let go!" Papa G shrieked and tried to swat O'Meara away.

The detective grabbed a fistful of the big man's T-shirt, which was torn and in pieces, but quickly realized he was hanging on to a pouch, not the shirt.

Papa G's eyes, knotted with fear, jerked from O'Meara to the prize in his hand. "Let go!" he repeated furiously, barely able to keep his head above water.

"Okay," O'Meara shot back and, with the pouch firmly in his grip, tore it away as he pushed off the big man and made for a rooftop nearby.

He pulled himself atop the roof and then turned, searching downstream for the Haitian.

Papa G bobbed to the surface several yards away, his rangy body no longer an asset but a flailing crutch, and then disappeared.

O'Meara, exhausted but jubilant, was surprised to see the Haitian shoot to the surface once more, farther downstream still, his eyes wild with panic. His head crashed against a telephone pole with a sickening thud, but he had enough presence of mind to grab on to the pole and wrap it in a desperate bear hug. And there he clung for several seconds, until a crumbling shotgun shack, shaken loose from its foundation, thundered through the floodwaters straight at him, snapping the pole in half and taking Papa G down one last time.

CHAPTER 28

He woke with the sun blazing down on him. How long had he slept? He rolled over onto his side and stared off into the western sky, blocking out the sun with his left hand. Judging by the sun's position—and the heat coming off the black composition roof beneath him—it was late afternoon. The winds had died, and the floodwaters, before a raging river, had peaked, though they showed no signs of receding anytime soon. Aside from the dull rhythmic sound of a helicopter in the distance, the neighborhood was eerily quiet. New Orleans was finally at peace with itself.

Detective O'Meara ran a hand over his face and quickly drew it away, wincing. His right eye was swollen shut, and his mouth felt raw, inside and out. Having survived a hard run from the Super Dome to the Lower Nine, a bruising fight with Papa G, and a near drowning, he was parched to the bone. But he didn't dare drink from the fetid waters swirling around him.

He remembered the leather pouch, still clutched in his right hand, and carefully opened it. Inside was a small cloth doll, faceless and feeble-looking. This had been the source of Papa G's power? The detective smiled wryly. Maybe he should ask Esmeralda to fashion him one. He was just superstitious enough to respect the mystery behind it. After cutting off its head, he pulled the stuffing free and tossed the lot of it into the brackish floodwaters.

A house across the submerged street shifted on its foundations and then broke free, and O'Meara watched as it slowly picked up speed in the current, which, though relatively placid on the surface, was apparently still strong beneath. The house briefly came to rest against the canopy of a large sycamore before splitting in two, with one half staying put and the other rumbling on.

That was all the inspiration O'Meara needed to get moving. He slowly got to his feet, grimacing as he stood erect, and surveyed the surreal watery landscape, which looked the same in every direction. Cars hung in trees, houses were lodged against one another, and garbage floated by the tops of street signs peaking from beneath the black water. One particular item, however, caught his attention: a boat. Gleaming white in the bright sunlight and bobbing peacefully on the water, it was tethered to a covered garage two houses down.

O'Meara, wrinkling his nose at the toxic smell, slipped into the murky water, careful to keep his head above it, and swam the short distance to the boat, which, upon closer inspection, revealed itself to be a Sea Ray. As soon as he dragged himself aboard, he cut the line and then went to work starting the motor, which chugged to life on the first try.

"How do you like that?" O'Meara said with a smile.

Navigating by rooftops and the occasional street sign, the detective made his way toward the Edmondses' residence, but on the way to Jason's grandmother's place, he picked up three passengers: an African-American retiree, who had gotten trapped in his attic by the rising floodwaters and had been forced to hack his way through the roof with a hatchet; the old gentleman's droopy-eyed basset hound, which had to be repeatedly restrained from diving into the water and chasing after the steady stream of debris floating by; and a short-haired black cat, which, after being pried from the top of a small magnolia, had taken up residence beneath O'Meara's seat, getting as far from the overeager basset hound as it could.

"What's your name?" O'Meara asked his human passenger.

"Jules," the old man said, stroking his dog's head.

"You ever see anything like this before?"

"Not since I was a boy," Jules said with a self-deprecating smile, crow's feet appearing at the corners of his jaundiced eyes. "But they been talking about this for years. It had to come."

"It sure did."

As they floated down Jason's street, the detective spotted the kid and his grandmother atop her roof, where they were reclining on a blanket and enjoying the shade from an oversized beach umbrella. Jason stood and waved.

"Ahoy!" O'Meara hollered.

The high school sophomore hadn't lied about being prepared. Beside him sat a cooler, no doubt stocked with food and water, and a bulging duffel bag, presumably stuffed with a first-aid kit and other essentials.

"We need to get to Charity," Jason said calmly.

One look at Grandma Edmonds confirmed his diagnosis. She was shaky and bleary-eyed, and probably on the verge of a diabetic coma.

"Let's do it," O'Meara said and helped the boy ease his grandmother into the boat.

Once Grandma Edmonds was safely seated in the middle of the small boat, which was sitting significantly lower in the water now than it had been when O'Meara first commandeered it, the detective fired up the engine, and the ragtag group began their pilgrimage to Charity Hospital. On the way, they passed a logjam of brand new running shoes, ostensibly sprung loose by looters somewhere upstream, and were forced to navigate through clouds of dragonflies, which had come to feast on the swarms of mosquitoes and gnats gathering on the water's surface. Papa G had been right about the Apocalypse, although the exact details had eluded him, including the fact that he wouldn't live to see the hordes of water moccasins, tangled together and riding anything that floated, or the giant sewer rats, scrambling for dry land, or the dislodged cockroaches, suddenly homeless and taking wing. The surviving humans, young and old and nearly all of them shell-shocked, waded through a toxic stew on their way to higher ground, carrying whatever hadn't been swept away by the floodwaters. And as the sun went down over New Orleans, the sky a brilliant cobalt blue, a multitude of frogs sang a haunting lullaby to a captive audience.

EPILOGUE

"You all right?" Payton asked.

Detective O'Meara laughed softly. Although his sister was the one who had been buried alive, he felt like a part of him had died.

"Yeah," he said and touched his sister's hand, which was still hooked up to an IV. "How 'bout you?"

"I don't know," she said, almost dreamily. "I guess I'm wondering what else can go wrong, you know?"

As Blackendy had predicted, the floodwaters had taken out Charity Hospital's backup generators, leaving the hospital to swelter in the hurricane's humid aftermath. Across the street, Tulane University Medical Center, a private hospital, was being evacuated by helicopter. But Charity Hospital, ever the underdog, had been left to its own devices, abandoned during its direst hour. Even Billy was gone—he had left with Blackendy, the troublesome prisoner, who would soon be joining other miscreants at the Greyhound Bus Terminal, which was being converted into a makeshift prison. New Orleans, a city built below sea level, was sinking beneath the terrible weight of its own hubris. From the mayor on down, no one had prepared for the worst. And now here it was.

Demoralized and isolated, numerous police officers had gone AWOL, some of them even joining the looting. Valiant but understaffed efforts by the Coast Guard, meanwhile, were underway. There was no telling when—or *if*—federal help would arrive. In the meantime, pettiness and revenge were running loose in the Big Easy. Alongside reports of looting and the usual mayhem, stories began to circulate of rooftop rapes and "big dumps," creative deposits of human waste in bars, restaurants, and stores of all kinds.

"I still like New Orleans," Payton said, stifling a yawn. "But maybe I'll check the weather forecast before my next visit."

O'Meara slumped in his chair. He was relieved to know someone still cared about his adopted hometown, but at the moment, he was too tired to respond. He drifted off, vowing to himself that he would show his sister a better time if she ever came back.